SACRIFICE
REPORTING IN KABUL

6-2-14

SACRIFICE

REPORTING IN KABUL

CHARLIE KADADO

For Terri,

Best wishes —

Charlie Kadado

MOORE PUBLISHING

Copyright Information

This is a work of fiction. The names, characters, places and incidents are either the product of the author's imagination or are used fictitiously. Any resemblance to actual business establishments, events or locals is entirely coincidental.

For more information visit Moore Publishing at

MoorePublishingBooks.com

Also visit BookfieldCreativeminds.com

ISBN: 978-0-9846987-6-9

Library of Congress Control Number: 2012939774

Dedicated to
The strong men and women in uniform who defend our
freedom and the journalists who put their lives on the line to
bring the news into our living rooms.

1

"This is Stephen Cook, signing off."

There are times when I wish I'd simply stuck to the eleven o'clock news. Most journalists dream of securing that *special job*; that position that will see them in exotic locales, reporting on important world events. It wasn't until I took one of those elusive positions that I understood just what I'd left behind as a correspondent for the RBC affiliate in Detroit.

Finished with the broadcast, I checked my voicemail and hurried out of the station at eleven thirty. Outside, the frigid December wind wreaked havoc, penetrating every surface and seemingly imbuing the outdoors with a profound silence. The trees stirred sluggishly, the road was free of traffic. Racing towards my car in the hopes of staying warm, I must have been the fastest moving thing for miles around.

As the cold engine lurched, I set to checking my phone. Five unread emails, two missed calls. Eyeing the clock on the dash, I tucked it back into my pocket. It was Friday night. Those things would have to wait.

I was living in a small apartment downtown back then. Though somewhat cramped, it proved sufficient for my dog Max and I. As soon as I stepped through the door, Max came running up, lavishing me with his attention.

"How are you, boy?" I asked, bending down to pet him. "You're a sight for sore eyes, Max."

It was nearly 12:30 when I headed to bed that night. Max followed close behind, curling up at my feet. Looking back on it, that was the night before everything changed. The restfulness of my sleep that night seems almost ludicrous to me now when I reflect upon the great changes that would soon be upon me.

***

I awoke to the ringing of my phone. By the time I answered it, the caller had left four messages. It could only be one person.

"Wake up," said Jennifer in the first message. "I

know it's your day off, but a huge story just broke. The mayor is about to address city council about their budget plan. We can't afford to miss out on this. Do me a favor and record a voiceover for the story. Get it to me as soon as you can."

Jennifer, the producer, was one of the most dedicated journalists I knew. In fact, I might go so far as to say that she was *too* dedicated. The news, to her, was a sort of addiction; she simply wasn't herself if she didn't have a strong handle on all matters; both international and local.

The other messages, I felt confident, were full of potential talking points. I poured myself a bowl of cereal before listening to them and jotting down a few notes. It was then that I decided to check my email.

Jennifer had filled my inbox with messages; only upon wading through them did I discover something that made me take pause. There was an email in my inbox whose subject read *Employment Opportunity.* At first, I thought it spam and very nearly deleted it. Upon closer inspection however, it proved to come from a surprising sender-- RBC headquarters in New York City.

'Dear Mr. Cook,' it read. 'I hope that this message finds you well. I am writing to you in the hopes that you might consider a change of pace. We're seeking a qualified reporter to fill a brand-new position here at RBC headquarters, and we feel strongly that you'd be the right man for the job. If you're willing, I'd like to meet you here in New York, to discuss the particulars of the job. I've included a link at the end of this message through which you might reserve a plane ticket. Let me know when you're available and we can decide on a day to meet. I'm looking forward to hearing from you. Sincerely, David Sawyer-- President, RBC Broadcasting.'

I don't know that I can convey in words just how excited I felt at reading Mr. Sawyer's message. The dream of most every young journalist is to work for a main station. While I'd enjoyed my tenure at the Detroit affiliate, there was no question that New York's facilities would be a major promotion, however. I re-read the message multiple times to make certain that I hadn't received it in error.

Sacrifice: Reporting In Kabul   11

Abandoning my breakfast, I hastily reserved my plane ticket and replied to the email. 'Mr. Sawyer,' I wrote. 'I'm looking forward to meeting you.'

How it was that I managed to record the voiceover for the city council announcement despite my tremendous excitement is a mystery to me. I fumbled through my notes and threw together a voiceover using the software on my laptop, which I then emailed to Jennifer. Receiving nothing in the way of response from her, I knew that it had been executed to her satisfaction. I was now free to spend the rest of my weekend daydreaming about a future in New York City.

I decided to keep the news to myself. It was too early yet for me to say anything to my co-workers, and admittedly, the news was still such a shock to me that I could scarcely believe it was true. I decided to withhold any announcements until the details were better-known.

Days went by in this secretive fashion. After every broadcast, I found myself skirting talk of my new opportunity, regaling the crew instead with mundane anecdotes about my day-to-day life. I'd worked with these people very closely over the years however, and before long, I knew that they would catch wind of my secret.

I recall the afternoon when I was sent to cover a bank robbery downtown. My photographer and I piled our gear into the van and sped to the bank, where the robbery was taking place. As I stepped out of the van a group of stoic police officers formed a makeshift barrier outside the door, from which they relayed their presence to the robber. I'd gathered from my briefing that it was a hostage situation. How many hostages the man had taken was impossible to say, however.

In dramatic fashion, I reported on the story. The photographer quickly set up the camera and lined up a good shot as I put in my earpiece.

"Things are tense here in downtown Detroit, where a would-be bank robber has taken an unspecified number of hostages."

We continued shooting footage for some time, but were instructed by the folks at the station to stand by as the police sought to extricate the man. During this period, there came through my earpiece a familiar voice.

"That's some fine reporting. I can see why the guys at HQ have taken an interest in you. Good luck, Stephen."

I couldn't help but grin. The cat was out of the bag. "Thanks," I replied, unable to ascertain just whose voice I'd heard through the earpiece. The flurry of activity about me had made it difficult to tell. Nonetheless, I knew that most of my co-workers would likely follow-up with their own congratulations.

I became lost for a moment in recalling the kindness of the crew and the strong relationships I'd built with each of them over the years. I fell so deep into thought that I very nearly missed the action behind me.

"Stephen," said the photographer, "get ready, man!"

"Good news here in downtown Detroit, as the local police have succeeded in infiltrating the bank. No shots have been fired, and it appears that this debacle may end without violence. We'll be certain to fill you in

on the details as they become available. This is Stephen
Cook, for RBC news."

***

It was at one of Dave's morning meetings that
the rest of the crew learned about the offer I'd received
from the main station. "Stephen here may be on to
bigger and better things!" he announced, swinging his
mug of coffee about with flourish. "I hear he's heading
out to New York to have a talk with the guys at the main
station. Is there any truth to that, Stephen?"

I nodded. "I received an email from HQ, yeah. I
don't know what'll come of it, but--"

"Nonsense," he blurted out. "They're going
to offer you a job, I'm quite sure. You're a stand-up
guy, Stephen. One of our best." Everyone in the room
launched into congratulations while Dave went on. "The
rest of you however, aren't nearly so lucky. The ratings,
people! We've got to up the ratings!"

From time to time, Dave would call these
morning meetings to discuss the current ratings. He

was a great guy with a sharp sense of humor who was willing to go to great lengths to improve the ratings. He'd gone so far as to interrupt our broadcasts to plead with the audience. "Thanks for watching our show," he'd once said during a morning broadcast, taking a seat next to one of the anchors. "I'm the general manager here at RBC Detroit, and I'd just like to ask that you continue watching our show. In fact, tell all of your friends about it. I need to earn a salary, after all." For all of his eccentricities, he proved a capable and friendly manager.

The morning meeting degenerated into a discussion of my offer, and I was assailed with questions.

"When are you headed out there?" Dave asked.

"I'll be meeting with the president in just a few weeks. Late January."

Dave laughed. "Meeting with the president? Well, isn't that something. You know, I've worked here longer than any of you and I've only ever met him but twice."

My co-workers proved extremely supportive. Although they expressed sadness at talk of my transferring, they unanimously congratulated me and wished me well. During such discussions, I couldn't help but air my doubts. Perhaps I wouldn't have the experience to take on such a job? They all assured me that I was an ideal candidate however, urging me to take the trip and meet with the president. Speaking to them, I couldn't help but feel sentimental. Their kindness and patience with me over the years had helped me become a more able journalist. I owed them a debt that I could not easily profess with words. It took some time, however I slowly came to realize just how much I'd miss working with the supportive Detroit crew. There was no telling what sort of people worked at the New York station. I could only hope that they'd be half as friendly and helpful as my co-workers at RBC Detroit.

In the days prior to my departure, I set to packing my bags. My stay wouldn't be an especially long one, however I wanted to make certain that I was fully prepared to make a good impression. I picked out my clothes ahead of time, matching shirts and ties.

I ironed my pants and placed them carefully into my valise. I also prepared a digital portfolio of my work by compiling clips of my anchoring and reporting in Detroit. Making such preparations relieved me somewhat of the strain of anticipation. Ironing my clothes; packing away my toiletries. I felt, in some small way, that I was making progress by setting myself up for success. Going through the motions proved quite soothing to me, as I struggled to understand the life changes I would soon be presented with.

The days flew by. It wasn't long before I found myself in late January, making the drive with Max to my uncle Jim's house in the suburbs. I hadn't seen him in some time; he'd grown somewhat haggard since I'd last seen him, however his face lit up as I bounded up onto the porch with Max's leash in hand.

"It's good to see you, Stephen. How have you been?"

"I'm doing well, uncle Jim. Thanks. How are you?"

He wrapped me in a brief hug. "Ah, well.

You know how it is with me. Same old, same old. Is everything ready for the big trip?"

"Yeah," I replied, "I did all of my packing in advance. I didn't want to forget anything."

"Good, good. How long did you say you'd be gone?"

"About a week. Give or take a few days. Don't worry, I'll make sure not to leave this needy mutt on your hands too long," I said, handing over the leash.

"Max is no trouble at all!" he said, kneeling to pet the dog. "He's a sweetheart, and I like the extra company."

I brought my uncle a container of dog food from the car and explained to him how much Max needed to eat each day. He brought Max into his back yard. "I think he'll like running out in the yard," my uncle said.

"I'm sure he will. We live in that cramped little apartment. He doesn't get an opportunity to run around outdoors as often as I'd like."

I said goodbye to Max and headed to the driveway with my uncle.

"Take care, Stephen. New York's a big city, you know."

"I know it, uncle Jim. Thanks for everything."

"No problem," he replied. "Just remember one thing. Those guys in New York may offer you a great job. And, if it's what you really want, then you should take it. Trust your heart though, Stephen. Your heart will never steer you wrong. Don't feel pressured into anything, no matter who's making the offer, alright?"

I nodded. "I'll make sure of it, uncle Jim. Thanks."

***

Upon arriving at the airport, I found several flights had been delayed. Peering through the massive windows in the airport lobby, it was clear to see why. Several runways had been obscured with freshly fallen snow. I inquired with one of the clerks about my flight.

"No, it seems that your flight is still on schedule.

This snow came out of nowhere, but it ought to clear up somewhat in the next few hours. You're in luck."

I dropped off my bags and went through airport security before sitting down outside my gate to read the local newspaper. I wondered what sort of local papers New York had; if their brand of journalism was anything like I'd encountered in Detroit. When I was finished reading the paper, I tucked it under my arm and waited to board the plane. I'd bring it along with me; a memento from faraway Detroit.

When the time came to board, I ambled nervously to my seat. I peered out the window at the runway, my heart swollen both with excitement and a vague melancholy I could not quite trace. This trip was an important one; a life-changing one. The captain greeted us overhead and the plane took off shortly thereafter. I let out a sigh as snowy Detroit became more and more distant beneath us.

I'd studied at the University of Michigan, majoring in journalism; I'd worked seven years at the RBC affiliate in Detroit. And finally, at twenty-thousand feet, I came to understand why. Those years of work and experience had been preparation for this moment. I'd spent those years dreaming about new, exciting opportunities, and finally, such opportunities were upon me. I leaned into the plush seat. This was what dreams were made of.

2

"We're approaching JFK International Airport," said the captain overhead. "Welcome to New York City. Current temperature is an icy six degrees Fahrenheit, and there appears to be about eight inches of snow on the ground. We'll be landing shortly. We ask that you remain in your seats during this time and we thank you for flying with us."

The announcement roused me from a deep sleep. I'd spent the bulk of the flight slumped over in my seat, peering out through the window at the world passing by beneath us. At some point, I'd been overcome by a tremendous fatigue, and had slept soundly for the remainder of the trip. Whereas the scene outside the window had been bright during the day, the sky was marked now with an inky darkness. Rubbing at my eyes, I tried to discern the land beneath us through the night.

My stomach rumbled noisily. Having slept the whole trip, I hadn't had the opportunity to eat anything.

I stretched and looked out into the aisle, hoping to alert one of the hostesses. They'd all shuffled to their stations for the landing however, and probably wouldn't be able to give me something to snack on. I'd have to find something to eat at the airport.

I had never visited an airport at 11:30 PM before. As a result, I was quite surprised to find it bustling. The baggage claim area was filled with impatient folk and the hallways were nigh unnavigable in places. For a brief time, I forgot my hunger and forced my way through the arrival process. Finally, a few minutes after midnight, I managed to escape the busy airport and get my first proper look at New York City.

Hauling my bags across the sidewalk, I was assaulted by an icy breeze. Each gust brought with it flecks of snow, the passage of which reddened my skin. I pulled the collar of my coat tight and prepared to hail a taxi. Ambling down the length of the sidewalk however, I caught sight of something most peculiar.

There stood a shivering man with a sign a short distance from the airport entrance. "Stephen Cook," it read.

"Excuse me," I said, wandering towards the man. "My name is Stephen Cook."

"From Detroit?" he asked, setting down the sign.

"That's right."

"Great, let me help you with your bags," he said, motioning towards a snowy cab beside the curb.

Together we loaded the bags into the trunk and got into the car. "Thanks," I told him, brushing away the snowflakes that clung to my hair. "Did the people from the station send you?"

"That's right," he said, cranking up the heat. "I've been waiting out there for about an hour now. I was starting to wonder if you'd ever show up!"

"I'm sorry," I replied. "It's so cold out. The airport was quite crowded, though."

"It's no problem. What's a little snow and ice, eh?" He slowly left the side of the curb and maneuvered into traffic. "The streets are kind of a mess, so thankfully traffic's not too heavy. I'll have you to your hotel in no time."

"I'm glad to hear it. Which hotel is it?"

"It's only a few minutes away from here, a pretty nice place."

He drove slowly through the snow-laden streets, careful not to swerve into the nearby cars with each turn. We came upon a small car accident, which slowed us down a bit. While stopped and awaiting the instructions of a traffic officer, my stomach began once more to growl.

"Goodness, you sound hungry," said the cab driver as I rubbed at my stomach.

"Ah, well, I haven't had an opportunity to eat today," I said, feeling somewhat embarrassed.

"I see. Well," he replied, rummaging about in his passenger seat, "do you like chocolate?"

I smiled. "I do."

He handed me a candy bar. "Eat up, then. I don't

want you passing out in my cab," he laughed.

"Are you sure? How much do I owe you?" I asked, reaching for my wallet.

"Oh, no charge Mr. Cook. The guys at the station have compensated me rather well for this trip. It's on the house."

I nibbled at the chocolate while watching the snow saunter through the air all about us. Eventually, the traffic officer let us pass, and we began once more through the frigid streets. A few minutes later, we arrived at the Sheraton hotel.

"Here we are, the Sheraton," said the cab driver. "If you'll step out, I'll bring your bags into the lobby."

The lobby was warm and well-lit. The cab driver hauled my luggage into the lobby and, after a brief farewell, piled back into his cab and disappeared into the streets. I took my things and approached the front desk, which was manned by a single young woman.

"Hello, miss. My name is Stephen Cook. I believe I have a reservation here?"

"Oh, yes. We've been waiting for you, Mr. Cook. Your room was reserved a few days ago; suite 310." She asked me for my ID and began filling out various forms. "This weather is really something else, isn't it?"

"It sure is," I replied.

She handed me a room key and gave me directions to suite 310. I thanked her and hopped onto the elevator. The hotel seemed quite nice. I was flattered somewhat that the folks at RBC had put me up in such a place. They could have just as easily saved some money by sending me to a Holiday Inn. "I could get used to this," I mumbled to myself with a laugh.

I sought out my room on the third floor and opened the door. Flipping on the lights, I was met with a rather welcoming sight. The room's décor was of a pleasant sort, and I could tell that the room had been freshly cleaned. Bolting the door behind me, I set aside my bags and explored further. The bathroom boasted a large bathtub as well as a shower stall. A nice television had been positioned across from the bed, and spare pillows and blankets had been set aside for me on the dresser. Upon them, I found a note.

'Please enjoy your stay, Mr. Cook,' it read. My gaze lingered somewhat on the signature beneath it; it was that of RBC president David Sawyer. It was a thoughtful gesture. Taken aback by the warmness of my welcome, I set the note on my nightstand and took off my shoes. The bed proved every bit as comfortable as it had seemed. I set an alarm and drifted off into a peaceful sleep.

***

The sun had not yet risen when the alarm clock began to blare. I switched it off and looked out groggily at the room, which was bathed in darkness. Somehow, I didn't feel completely rested. Nonetheless, I soldiered out of bed and flipped on the lights. It was going to be a busy day, and I'd need an early start.

I phoned room service and ordered a light breakfast. By the time I'd finished showering at 7 AM, it had arrived. I watched a bit of the morning news while eating, and then set to making myself look presentable. Smoothing out the sleeves of my suit jacket, I looked myself over in the mirror.

I'd set up an appointment with Mr. Sawyer for 9:30. Although traffic would probably be dense, I anticipated that it would only take me about thirty minutes to make it to the main station from the hotel. I asked the clerk working at the front desk to make certain, and they assured me that RBC headquarters was, even on the busiest of days, a mere twenty-five minutes away. Feeling confident, I threw on my jacket and left the hotel. Waiting for me outside, was another cab.

"Stephen Cook?" the driver asked, peering out at me from inside the cab.

"Yes?"

"Come on in, sir. I've been sent here to bring you to the RBC station."

I got into the cab and we drove through the freshly-plowed streets towards the station. At some point in the night the snowfall had ceased. The bitter cold yet persisted, however.

"Traffic's been a beast this morning because of the snow. I'll get you to where you need to go in time, though. I know a quicker route."

We drove through a series of side streets, some of which had not yet been cleared of snow. The cab driver, confident in his skills, managed to keep his promise however. We arrived at the station at about 8:45-- with forty-five minutes to spare before my meeting with Mr. Sawyer.

"Thanks for the ride," I said, stepping out of the taxi.

The building was gorgeous. Although not the largest building in the area, it was far larger than any building I'd ever worked in before. It looked to be several stories high, and its exterior had been well-maintained. Groups of locals and tourists were huddled outside despite the cold, peering through the windows to watch the segments of the morning show as they were taped.

I entered and made my way to the front desk.

"Good morning. How can I help you?" asked the

secretary.

"My name is Stephen Cook, I've got a meeting at 9:30 with Mr. David Sawyer."

She flipped through a log book. "Yes, I see that. If you could just have a seat over there, he'll be with you shortly."

I complied and walked over the the seating area.

"Oh, and feel free to help yourself to a cup of coffee if you like," she called out after me.

There was a small coffee station in the seating area. I nodded to her and poured myself a cup before plopping down on one of the plush seats.

I'd scarcely begun to sip at my coffee when someone called out to me.

"Stephen Cook?"

I turned. "Yes?"

A tall man in a tailored black suit stood beside the front desk. He approached me with a smile. "Hello,

Mr. Cook. My name is David Sawyer."

I stood and extended my hand to him. "It's a pleasure to meet you Mr. Sawyer."

He looked me in the eye intensely as we shook hands. "No, Mr. Cook. The pleasure's all mine, I assure you. All of us are excited at the prospect of your potential employment here."

"Thank you." Mr. Sawyer seemed a rather personable individual. His voice was smooth and calm; it seemed to me the sort of professional voice that had been honed and perfected through years of intense practice. Perhaps he'd worked as an anchor for the news in the past? I followed him from the lobby to the elevator, where we traveled to the second floor.

"My schedule cleared up a bit this morning. The secretary told me you'd arrived, so I thought it better not to keep you waiting. I'd like to show you something, Mr. Cook." The elevator door gave way with a click, revealing to me a bustling studio. "This is Studio A."

I followed him through the studio, marveling

at the facilities. "Goodness," I said. "This place is enormous! It's much bigger than the Detroit station's studio."

He placed a finger to his lips and whispered a reply. "Yes, this is quite an upgrade." He motioned towards the corner of the studio, where the morning show was currently being taped.

"Ben Roberts and Debra Martin?" I uttered, somewhat starstruck. The two anchors, Ben and Debra, were among my favorite national anchors.

"That's right," replied Mr. Sawyer. "Would you like to meet them?"

The two of us walked to the corner and watched the broadcast from the sidelines. During one of the commercial breaks, I was able to meet both of the anchors. I made a fool of myself, professing to them how fond I was of their work. They were polite and expressed interest in hearing that I might possibly take a position at the main station.

Prior to visiting the station, it had never occurred

to me that I might have the opportunity to work with such a talented team. I'd idolized these anchors; the prospect of working alongside them was almost too good to be true.

I followed Mr. Sawyer back onto the elevator, where we rose to the top floor and walked to his office. He offered me a chair in front of his massive desk, and the two of us began looking through my portfolio. All the while, he expressed enthusiasm with my work, and noted that he'd heard great things about me from the folks at the Detroit station. I handed him a copy of my resume, which he studied with great interest as well.

"For a man of your age, you've got an impressive resume, Stephen."

"Thank you for saying so."

He set aside the resume and began to describe the new position in more detail. "I've been in talks with various of the network's administrators, and I feel strongly that you'd be a good fit for the position of North American Correspondent. Such a position would entail gathering facts and reporting on stories throughout the

US and Canada."

"That sounds wonderful," I said. "It's the sort of position I've always wanted."

He smiled. "So I imagine that means you're interested? In any case, here's a file containing more information on this opportunity. Read through it to familiarize yourself with the particulars." He peered at his wristwatch. "Ah, it's just about time for lunch. Are you hungry, Stephen? We've got a cafeteria downstairs, and the food's actually quite good. It'll be my treat."

I agreed, and the two of us left the office. Along the way, Mr. Sawyer called out to a man in an adjacent room. "This is Gary Williams. He's the vice-president here at RBC."

Mr. Williams extended a hand. "You're Stephen Cook, I presume? It's a pleasure."

I shook his hand. "It's nice to meet you."

The three of us took the elevator down to the first floor and made our way to the cafeteria. The facilities had only just opened, which meant we could sit wherever we liked. I ordered a small lunch and joined the two administrators at a large table near the center of the cafeteria. The food, like Mr. Sawyer had said, was quite good.

"Your credentials are impressive," said Mr. Williams, slurping up a spoonful of soup. "You've accomplished a lot as a young journalist. That kind of work ethic is a rare thing."

Mr. Sawyer nodded in agreement. "I'll say. I know people who've been in this business twice as long as Stephen here, and who've accomplished half as much."

It was somewhat difficult, listening to their constant praise. Not because I disliked it; it was true that I'd worked hard over the years and that I was happy to have my service acknowledged, but because it wasn't something I was used to. For the bulk of the meal, I listened to the two of them talk, too shy to interject very much.

As time passed, other staff members entered the cafeteria to order their lunches. From time to time, Mr. Sawyer would call over crew members and introduce them to me. They all proved quite friendly, reminding me somewhat of the fine folks I worked with in Detroit. I felt relieved as I met the New York crew, knowing that I'd fit in quite well.

After lunch, the two administrators excused themselves, but thanked me for my time. "I'll be talking with the rest of the higher-ups about hiring you, Stephen. I'll probably get ahold of you later tonight, in fact. Keep an eye out for a message," said Mr. Sawyer.

I left the studios around 2 PM, and walked a short distance towards a Starbucks, eager to read through the file Mr. Sawyer had given me. I ordered a small coffee and found myself a cozy corner to sit in. Prying the lid from my coffee cup, I began reading through the file.

The file began with an introduction. "The energy of the mind is the essence of life," it read. It went on to thank me for my interest, and asked that I keep an open mind whilst reading about the position.

The next page detailed the particulars of the position that Mr. Sawyer had previously touched upon during our meeting. I read through this section at a furious pace, thrilled with all of the new opportunities that had been presented to me. I took a sip of my coffee and began reading about the job's pay. My salary as a North American Correspondent would be in the ballpark of $250,000-- more than double what I was making in Detroit. Although the money had never been my main focus, I was a bit awestruck to see such a large number.

I finished reading through the file and tucked it away excitedly. A few hours had passed, and I decided to go out for a nice dinner. I left the cafe and hailed a cab.

"Do you know of any good Italian restaurants around here?" I asked the cabbie as I got into the back seat.

"There are several," he said. "If you don't have anything in particular in mind, I'll drop you off at my favorite," he replied. "It's about five minutes from here."

"Sounds good." I watched the city roll by through the window. There was no reigning in my imagination; the experiences I'd had in meeting the New York crew, touring the station and learning about my new opportunity had been too surreal to process. I enjoyed a large dinner that night in utter bliss.

I received a text message from Mr. Sawyer at around 7 PM, telling me that a taxi would be waiting for me outside of the hotel at 6 AM. 'Tomorrow's going to be another early day,' I thought to myself. I retired to my hotel and, setting my alarm, drifted off to sleep.

3

I was in the cab by about 5:30 AM. My excitement served to expel whatever fatigue remained from a short night's sleep, and I chatted happily with the groggy cab driver. Upon my arrival to the studio, I checked in at the front desk and was escorted by the secretary to the studio. Mr. Sawyer met me near the elevator.

"Good morning, Stephen. Are you excited for the broadcast?"

"I am," I replied, taking my seat.

I watched as the anchors reviewed their scripts. All about the studio, people were going frantically through the motions; the meteorologist updated his graphics, the producer gave orders to the crew in the control room, the sound crew did several sound checks. Somehow, from this chaos, a flawless newscast was carried out only moments later.

"RBC This Morning starts now," said one of the anchors.

I'd started my day with those same words each morning. In Detroit, no matter the shift I was working, I would wake up to watch the news as a means of preparing myself for the day to come. Munching on breakfast, I'd heard that opening line countless times.

The broadcast went off without a hitch. The anchors delivered their lines flawlessly, and everything seemed to go according to plan. I was a bit intimidated by their professionalism, to be honest. I wondered briefly whether I'd be able to perform to that same standard. Such professionalism is a learned behavior, however. In time, I'd become skilled enough to work in such an environment.

After the show ended, I had an opportunity to meet with the anchors and producer. The producer was jovial, happy to have completed the broadcast. I could sense the relief in his voice as he spoke to me.

"So," I overheard one of the crew members say to the producer, "what do you think about this segment for tomorrow morning?"

I was floored. The show had only just ended, and

already the crew was planning their next broadcast. In Detroit, we didn't worry about the next day's show until it actually arrived!

I turned to Mr. Sawyer. "Are they really preparing for the next broadcast? Already?"

"They sure are," he said, somewhat amused. "Is that surprising?"

"It is. In Detroit, we do things a little differently. We don't usually plan so far in advance."

"I see. Well, we have our own way of doing things around here. The producers prefer to prepare content for the broadcasts in advance. We've found that the show runs much more smoothly that way. The news is a temperamental thing, after all. Doing things in this way allows us to avoid some of those variables that might otherwise complicate things during our broadcasts."

I wasn't sure what to say. Sensing my nervousness, Mr. Sawyer assured me. "I know that this is quite different for you. Don't worry though, Stephen.

You've done great work in Detroit, and I'm sure that, with a little help, you'll catch on in no time. You may even find that you prefer to work in this way."

"Maybe so," I replied.

The two of us left the studio and went to his office. "Have you had a chance to look over those papers I gave you?" he asked as he took a seat.

"I've read most of them, yes."

"Good," he said. "So, what are your impressions?"

"Well," I began, "I've got to be honest, this sounds like my dream job, Mr. Sawyer. I've watched the New York broadcasts for many years, and I've dreamt of working with your talented staff. I'd be lying if I said I wasn't a little nervous, but I find this whole thing to be very exciting. To be honest, I feel like it's a little too good to be true-- as though it's all a dream."

He laughed. "Well, I assure you that it isn't a dream. At least, not in the sense you're talking about. But, so far as your aspirations go, this is a dream that could very well come true, Stephen. I'd like for us to meet again tomorrow. You can tour the rest of the building and perhaps meet a few of the other correspondents."

"That sounds wonderful."

"I don't want you to rush into this position, Stephen. I want to make sure you're comfortable with everything here in New York. I know that this could be a big change for you, and it's in your best interest to choose what works best for you. Although we'd be devastated if you decided to stay in Detroit, we'd all understand."

"Thank you for your consideration, Mr. Sawyer. I appreciate that."

I left the office and returned to my hotel, where I spent the remainder of the day in speculation. If offered the job, would I take it? The job seemed like a great fit; a wonderful way to build my resume and move up in the world of Journalism. But would it make me happy? I settled into bed early that night, hoping that the morning might bring with it some clarity.

***

The next morning, I arrived at the studio in the hopes of meeting with some of the correspondents. I was informed at the front desk however, that there'd been a slight change. I was expected not by Mr. Sawyer, but by Tom Clark, the Chief North American correspondent. He approached me at the desk and the two of us began a brief tour. Along the way, he told me about various of the stories he'd had the opportunity to cover throughout the years.

He was an interesting guy; an eloquent speaker with a great sense of humor. I understood right away why it was that he'd been so successful. In the offices, he showed me some of the editing tools and computer programs used for their shows and clips of live coverage.

As the day wore on, I was caught up in thinking about just how fortunate I was to be presented with such an opportunity. At the end of the day, as Tom was saying goodbye, I received word that Mr. Sawyer wanted to speak with me. I took the elevator upstairs and entered his office.

"How are you, Stephen? I hope that your meeting with Tom went well."

"It did," I said, "He seems like a really nice guy."

"I'm glad. Please, take a seat," he said.

I sat down.

"Stephen, we've looked through your resume several times now, and we're very interested in hiring you. Something caught my eye during my last perusal, and I'd like to have a talk to you about it."

Was something wrong? My mind grew frenzied with worry.

He pulled a copy of my resume from his desk. "I see here that you speak Pashto?"

I nodded. "Oh, yes. I do."

"I see. Well, Stephen, I apologize for all of the confusion. You see, because of your abilities, we were wondering if you might be interested in filling a different position."

"A different position? What kind of position?"

"We've been seeking a foreign affairs correspondent to cover stories in Afghanistan. The job I'd like to offer you right now is not that of North American correspondent, but foreign correspondent, to be stationed in Kabul, Afghanistan."

My mind stalled out suddenly. I wasn't sure of what to make of his offer. At sixteen, my father had enrolled me in Pashto classes at the local university. As a Colonel in the US army who was fighting the war in Afghanistan, it wasn't too surprising. While initially I wasn't enthusiastic about learning Pashto, the more I learned about the culture and the language, the more disciplined I became. My father had always talked about me becoming a linguist; he understood the value in being multilingual, and thus urged me to learn as many languages as I could. "Someday," he'd always tell me, "this is going to benefit you. You'll thank me someday." Sure enough, he'd been right.

The possibility of being stationed in Kabul was

both exciting and terrifying to me. Although I spoke

the right language and felt confident in my skills as a

journalist, I wasn't at all certain that such a job would

be fulfilling to me. That type of journalism was unlike

anything I'd ever experienced. I wanted nothing more at

that moment than to return to my hotel and make a list of

pros and cons about the offer. Only then did I feel that I

could make a decision.

"We would offer you a salary of $350,000 a year,"

said Mr. Sawyer, interrupting my thoughts. "This is a big

opportunity." He handed me a thick filed folder filled with

papers. "Please read through this file and let me know

what you think."

"I will," I said, taking the file.

"I told you before, Stephen. I don't want to

pressure you into this job. I will need your decision

by tomorrow evening, however. This is a position that

needs filled as soon as possible. Please look through

those papers and get back to me."

***

In my hotel room that evening, I began reading through the massive file. I felt overwhelmed by the new offer, but was reminded by the title page to 'keep an open mind'. I did my best to do so.

"The following file details an employment opportunity in Kabul, Afghanistan as a foreign affairs correspondent. The duties of such a correspondent include finding, collecting and reporting on stories about the current state of Afghanistan. You will be RBC's source for all political information in the country. Furthermore, you will be RBC's source for all news pertaining to the ongoing war. Enclosed are details about lodging, safety and working conditions."

The remaining documents outlined the duties I'd be responsible for in Afghanistan. My crew would be comprised of six members; two photographers, a technician, a security advisor, a personal assistant and myself. For every six months spent in Kabul, I would be awarded a monetary raise of $10,000. The documents designated the Kabul Serena Hotel as my place of lodging, and noted that many journalists in Afghanistan chose to stay there.

I was certainly interested in the position. There were a few reservations I had that kept me from calling up Mr. Sawyer and accepting the job forthwith, however. Was I ready to leave the United States? Was I willing to immerse myself in the culture of another country for my job?

I reviewed the documents once more. There was no limit to the time I could spend in Afghanistan, however they hoped that I would choose to stay there at least one year. I knew that I'd have to go with my heart on this offer, however I went to sleep that night, uncertain of what my heart really wanted.

I paid Mr. Sawyer a visit the next morning without a decision in mind.

"This is a wonderful opportunity you've provided me with, Mr. Sawyer. I must confess that I'm not altogether certain that I should accept, however. I don't know that I'm ready to leave the United States. Although I love working for RBC and would very much enjoy working for the main station, I'm not sure that I want to dedicate myself to RBC in this way."

"I understand," Mr. Sawyer replied. "I understand exactly where you're coming from, Stephen. However, it's important that you make a decision before returning to Detroit. Please think about it all you like. Weigh the advantages and disadvantages of the position. Do what you must. But I need an answer."

"Well, Mr. Sawyer, it's a difficult thing to do. I've always been one to follow my dreams, but at the same time, I've got a lot going on in the United States. I have a dog named Max who relies on me, and my entire family lives here as well. Am I to just leave all of them behind? What would I do about that?"

"Yes, to put it simply. You would have to leave a great and many things behind. Admittedly, we can do some things to accommodate you, Stephen. We have another correspondent by the name of Roger Spencer in Kabul who took his dog with him. If you like, we could certainly make arrangements for Max in Kabul as well."

I laughed. They'd really thought this out.

"We can give you a while longer to consider this offer," he said.

I pondered for a brief while before replying. "You know what, Mr. Sawyer? I think I'll just follow my heart."

Slowly and steadily, I signed the contract that would send me to Kabul.

The cab ride to the hotel was a difficult one. I felt nauseous with unease, and wasn't sure if I'd done the right thing. Nonetheless, my excitement prevailed and I retired for the night, my mind reeling with the possibilities that lay before me.

***

I flew back to Detroit the next day and headed to my uncle Jim's house. As I approached the door, Max erupted into a fit of barking.

"Hey, welcome back Stephen," said my uncle, opening the door. Max followed close behind, leaping in the air with joy. "As you can see, Max here has missed you," he added with a laugh.

"Hey, uncle Jim. You'll never believe this. The guys at RBC offered me a job-- I've signed up to work as a foreign correspondent in Kabul, Afghanistan!"

He looked stunned. "In Afghanistan?"

"Yeah," I replied.

"No kidding! That's really something, Stephen."

I smiled. "I have to be honest; the shock is still setting in. I'm not sure whether or not I made the right decision. It's a great opportunity, the pay is good and it's a huge upgrade from my current job in Detroit. But I still don't know."

"Well, did you follow your heart?" my uncle asked.

"I tried my best to, yeah. I remembered what you told me, and I made sure not to rush into anything. The folks at the station were pretty understanding."

"Then you're fine, Stephen. Your heart will never steer you wrong. Hey," he said, "have you talked to your parents?"

"Not yet, no."

"Go and give 'em a call, then! I'm sure they'll be excited to hear the news."

I stepped into the kitchen and picked up the phone. My parents had moved out of Detroit to California upon my dad's retirement from the army. I dialed their number nervously.

"Hello," my mother answered.

"Hey, mom. It's me, Stephen."

"Hello, sweetheart, how are you?"

I paused. "I'm good mom. I'm good. I just got back from New York City. I met with the guys at the main RBC station."

"Oh? That sounds exciting. Did everything go well?"

"It went much better than expected, actually." I laughed. "Is it alright if I talk to dad for a minute?"

"Sure thing, honey." She set down the phone and sought out my father.

"Hello, Stephen," he said.

"Hey, dad. How are you?"

"I'm fine. What's this I hear about you going to New York?"

"I met with the folks at the main station, dad. They've offered me a really good job."

"No kidding? What sort of job?"

"You'll never believe this," I laughed, "I've accepted a job in Kabul. They saw that I spoke Pashto and wanted me to work as a foreign correspondent."

My dad laughed heartily. "Now isn't that something! I told you that Pashto would come in handy some day, didn't I? I always told you you'd thank me for it in the future! That's exciting. I'm proud of you."

"Thanks, dad. And, yeah, looking back on it now, I'm glad you insisted on the Pashto classes."

My father took a moment to fill my mother in on the details. She returned to the phone some moments later. "Congratulations, sweetheart. That sounds very exciting!" As I knew she would, her attention soon turned to the less desirable aspects of the job. "I wonder-- will it be a safe job, honey?"

"I imagine so, yes. They'll have me working with a crew the whole time. Among them will be a security advisor. I wouldn't worry too much, mom."

"Well, I'm glad to hear that," she replied. "If it isn't too much trouble, we'd like to come out and visit you in Detroit in the next few days. Are you busy?"

"Not at all, mom. I'd like that. Just let me know when you guys plan on arriving."

After talking a while longer with my uncle Jim, Max and I returned to my apartment. I unpacked and set to writing a letter of resignation to Dave, the Detroit station's general manager. I stuffed it into an envelope and drifted off to sleep.

The next day, I headed to the station. "Good afternoon," I told the gate attendant. As he let me into the station, I was reminded of just how much I'd miss everybody in Detroit. Even the attendant would be missed.

I entered the station and made a beeline for the general manager's office. Placing the letter on his desk, I met with a few of my co-workers and informed them of my decision. Word spread like wildfire. In typical journalistic fashion, the crew began to investigate, asking me questions about the new job. They were all in awe as I described to them my time in New York.

Jennifer, the producer, was about to leave the station when she heard the news. "Stephen, what's all this gossip about? Are you really leaving us?"

"I am," I replied. "I'm going to work as a foreign correspondent in Kabul for the main station."

She smiled. "Man, what a job." She wished me luck, but reminded me that everyone at the Detroit station was a family. "Don't go forgetting about us now."

Later, I got a call from Dave. "I just read your letter Stephen. I'm not going to say that I'm not disappointed to see you go, but all the same I wish you luck. I'm happy for you. We'll talk more later."

I anchored the 6 PM news, and spent the remainder of the evening talking with my co-workers. They urged me to announce my resignation during the

11 o'clock broadcast. I also received an email from Mr. Sawyer, which contained further details about my new position. Apparently, I'd be shipping off for Kabul in March. I had less than a month left in the U.S.

I closed the 11 PM newscast by informing the viewers of my decision. The instantaneous outpouring of support on my Twitter page moved me. I hadn't ever realized just how much the whole city meant to me, and just how many people had relied on me for their news each day. I realized that it was for this reason; for the support and kindness of the viewers, that I'd worked so hard over the years to produce quality news reports.

Over the next few weeks, the folks at the station made a big deal about my departure. My tenure at the station was celebrated in various ways; they featured a few stories about my time working in Detroit. More than that however, one of their gestures sticks out in my mind above all the others. While anchoring, I was told that there was a breaking news story.

I read it off of the teleprompter. "We have some breaking news from downtown Detroit. RBC anchor

Stephen Cook will be stepping down from his position." I paused for a moment, realizing just what I'd read. The news was about me. From the studio, various of the crew members entered the set with balloons and cakes, and our celebration was featured in the tail end of the broadcast. I was moved very nearly to tears; they'd gone to great lengths to ensure that my farewell was a memorable one. Their thoughtfulness was inspiring.

During the 11 PM broadcast that same night, I began with my usual introduction. "Good evening, Detroit." As I did so however, I noticed others speaking the line in unison. Confused, I peered about the set, where I found my parents standing behind me. I welcomed them both with a hug and introduced them briefly to the viewers before continuing with the newscast.

I finished the broadcast and left the set to give them another hug.

"It's good to see you guys," I said.

"It's good to see you too, Stephen. We were interested in seeing you on the job. We asked Dave if it would be alright for us to attend the broadcast."

Dave smiled at me and walked over. "You should be very proud of Stephen here. He's a fine journalist. We're sad to see him go."

"We're very proud of him," my father replied. "He's always been a good kid."

My parents and I left the station and went to my apartment, where I set up a comfortable guest bed for them to sleep in. We spent some time discussing the new job, and I handed my dad the extensive file Mr. Sawyer had given me.

"This looks like a great job," he said to me as he perused the contents of the file. My mother agreed.

Exhausted, the three of us decided to talk about it more in the morning and settled into bed.

The next morning, we visited a local restaurant for breakfast. After ordering, our discussion continued.

"We're very happy for you," my mother said. "This is a once-in-a-lifetime opportunity."

"That's right," my father added. "This job could lead to even bigger and better things. Who knows; maybe you'll end up as one of their anchors in the future."

After our meal, we returned to my apartment, where my parents began to pack up their things. They were only able to spend a day in Detroit. I helped them with their bags and, after a long goodbye, they headed off to the airport.

***

My last day as an anchor in Detroit was filled with yet more celebrations. All over the internet, on several of RBC's websites, people wrote me nice messages. During the 6 PM show, my co-anchor interviewed me, asking me about my new position and about what I could expect in Afghanistan. Afterward, a brief montage of our favorite moments aired and we closed the broadcast with a hug.

The 11 o'clock show would be hardest for me, I realized. It was my final broadcast as an anchor at the Detroit station. I used the broadcast as an opportunity to extend my heartfelt gratitude to the viewers for their support. "Thank you for allowing me into your homes," I said, looking right into the camera. "Thank you, Detroit. Good night, Detroit. And good-bye, Detroit."

After the show, I cleared out my desk and drafted a quick note to Dave. Taking one last look around the station, I placed the note on Dave's desk and left.

"Thank you for everything you've done for me over the past few years," I'd written. "I'm so fortunate to have worked with you all. We've grown into a family over the years-- a family of dedicated news junkies. I hope to keep in contact with each and every one of you. Thanks for everything, Stephen."

4

My return to New York was much like my previous arrival; I slept most of the way and found my mind clouded with the possibilities of my new employment. After sleeping in a proper bed for a brief time, I left my hotel and headed for the main station, where I met the crew that would accompany me to Afghanistan.

Leaving the cab and entering the lobby, I found a small group sitting in the waiting area. The secretary pointed them out to me, and I went over to introduce myself.

"Hello, I'm Stephen Cook. I assume you folks are waiting for me?"

They began to introduce themselves immediately. I met Michael and Glenda, the photographers. They were pleasant, which was rather surprising considering the massive bag of gear they each shouldered. In their cases they carried large cameras as well as other pieces of important equipment. In all, I imagine their gear weighed about fifty pounds--

not at all the sort of load I could carry around easily for an extended period of time. They seemed to have little trouble with it as they introduced themselves however.

Daniel the technician introduced himself next. He, too, carried a massive load of equipment. Behind him was William, the security advisor. He explained to me his role, which was to keep the crew safe in the event of bombings or other dangerous events. Lastly, I met Ruth. Ruth was to be my personal assistant, and would assist me in obtaining interviews as well as covering some of my stories.

We shared a quick lunch at the station cafeteria and became better acquainted.

"How dangerous is it, the area where we'll be stationed?" I asked no one in particular.

"It's plenty dangerous. But that's why I'm coming along," said William, taking a sip of his cola. "You get used to it in no time, trust me."

It appeared that I was the only member of the crew that hadn't worked in Afghanistan. My inexperience made me feel somewhat apprehensive. Although the others were confident in their ability to work in such a setting, I wondered if I would be able to adapt. Would the other crew members think of me as a burden, rather than an asset? And further, would I be an easier target due to my inexperience?

William rummaged through his bag and handed me a packet full of safety information. "This ought to cover most everything, Stephen." He explained to me that he would be monitoring the situation in Afghanistan very closely. Upon the discovery of something dangerous, he would contact me through my IFB, or earpiece. The IFB would be connected both to the New York station's studio and to William, who would be surveying the scene from nearby. "It's true that this is a dangerous job. It's my top priority to protect you guys, though. The last thing we need is another dead journalist. I'll do my best to keep you folks safe; you guys just do your best to bring the news to the American people."

William went on to describe his extensive experience. He'd worked for decades in the region, protecting many correspondents over the years. There was little he hadn't experienced, and felt tremendously confident in his ability to seek out and expunge threats.

We chatted a while longer before heading upstairs to meet with Mr. Sawyer. He led us into a conference room, where we were met by numerous RBC administrators. They all thanked us for our service and wished us luck on our journey.

"We'd like to take this opportunity to thank you for your service to RBC. This is an important, difficult job. We're proud to employ such talented journalists, and we wish you the best of luck on your journey," said Mr. Sawyer.

Mr. Sawyer went on to discuss the methods we'd be using in Afghanistan in capturing the news. As he spoke, I felt my cell phone vibrate. I excused myself and answered the call in the hallway.

"Hey, Stephen," said my uncle Jim. "I was just calling to let you know that Max boarded the flight to France."

"I see. Thanks for letting me know, uncle Jim," I whispered.

"No problem. Good luck, Stephen. Stay safe."

"I will, uncle Jim. Thanks again."

I returned to the conference room, where Mr. Sawyer was explaining the correspondence system between Afghanistan and the New York station. "Your IFBs will be linked both to William and to the New York station. This will keep you safe, as well as provide us with a direct link to the story as its being taped."

He filled us in on the details of our departure, stating that we would be leaving in a day's time. "Tonight, we'll be putting you guys up in a local hotel. Tomorrow, you'll all be on your way bright and early. Best of luck."

After the meeting was over, I returned to my hotel and made certain that all of my things were packed. I secured my baggage and headed down to the hotel restaurant, where I ate a modest dinner.

I'd been impressed with the crew, and felt that I'd

be able to rely on them during my time in Afghanistan. I wondered as I ate what they were doing to prepare. Aside from Daniel, the technician, the other crew members all lived in or near New York. Until recently, Daniel had been working for a small news station in Georgia. Like me, he was still getting used to the hustle and bustle of a national station.

When my dinner was through I returned to my room and reviewed my boarding pass. Our initial flight would be spent in business class. We'd land in France, where we'd board a second, private flight. A cargo plane would be sent to France ahead of us, and would contain all of our equipment, which would then be loaded onto our private flight.

I watched a bit of TV before bed, wondering what life would be like in Afghanistan. I realized that I would only be in the United States for a while longer, and that life in Kabul would be extraordinarily different from my day-to-day life in America. It would likely be a long time before I'd be able to watch TV or eat American food again. There was a certain sadness to this realization.

***

It was just past 4 o'clock in the morning when I awoke. For whatever reason, I couldn't bring myself to sleep any longer. My mind had been addled with anticipation throughout the night, and I'd slept somewhat poorly as a result. Making the best of things, I choked down a quick bowl of cereal before beginning my morning routine. I showered and dressed quickly and carried my luggage down to the lobby. I ordered a coffee at the hotel restaurant and waited patiently for my fellow crew members to arrive.

One by one, they slowly met me in the hotel. Hauling their bags, they met me at my table and expressed their excitement. "I'm so excited," said Glenda. "I think you're really going to enjoy this trip, Stephen."

"I hope you're right," I laughed.

When the entire crew had arrived, we filed out of the hotel and hailed a pair of taxis. Loading up our belongings, we made haste to the airport. I'd left a few of my bags behind at the station, but had been assured by the staff that they'd be sent to me in a few days.

As we drove through the streets of New York for the final time, I found myself feeling rather melancholy. Everything around us was so typically American; the people, the cars, the buildings. I knew I'd miss it. How long would it be before I'd see such sights again? I leaned back in my seat and took in the scenery with enthusiasm. The one thing I didn't want to happen was for me to forget what things were like in my home country.

"Tell me," I asked William in the cab, "what's it like in Afghanistan? Do you get homesick often? Do you forget what America's like after you've been there a while?"

He laughed. "I used to get homesick, back when I first started. These days, I'm more comfortable with extended journeys like this one, though. Look out that window," he said, pointing at the skyscrapers all about us. "Doesn't matter where you go, Stephen. There's no way you'll ever forget scenery like this. What's more, I don't think it's possible to forget where you've come from." He showed me a pin on his jacket in the shape of an American flag.

"I'm glad to hear that," I said.

We arrived at the airport somewhat early. After going through airport security, we sat in the business lounge and discussed our trip prior to boarding.

"What do you like best about life in Afghanistan?" I asked Michael.

"The culture there is very interesting to me," he said. "I'm not sure what it is in particular. Maybe it's interesting to me simply because it's so different from our own. I tell you though; you never really understand where it is that you come from until you've experienced a completely different culture. Working in Afghanistan has given me a certain appreciation for where I come from. I guess that's my favorite aspect of life in Afghanistan-- it's broadened my horizons and taught me something about the world in general."

I rather liked his reasoning, and hoped that I, too, would gain such insights throughout the course of my journey.

After some time, we were finally able to board our flight. The attendant thanked us as we boarded. "Thank you for flying Air France. This is flight 128, bound for Paris. Thank you for your patronage." Another attendant walked the aisles of the plane, offering us drinks as we took our seats and made ourselves comfortable.

Each seat had access to a screen on which we could watch movies. Throughout the course of the flight I watched several movies, although I can't honestly recall which ones. I nodded off throughout them, awakened only occasionally by the passage of the attendants. Every few hours they'd pass through the aisles and offer the patrons drinks or snacks.

The meals on the flight weren't altogether bad. A business class meal was much better than anything I was used to on a plane, and was comprised of entrees like sirloin steak and grilled salmon. I had a steak, some mashed potatoes and a bit of baguette. 'It only makes sense that Air France should serve us baguettes,' I thought to myself with a smirk.

A few hours after our main meal, the attendants wheeled carts down the aisles stocked with sandwiches and soup, as though we were supposed to be hungry. Half-way through our flight most of us were stuffed. Not that that kept the attendants from offering us more food.

I began to wonder what Afghanistan would look like. I imagined small villages flanked by large, dusty mountains. Perhaps the terrain would be sandy and warm, basking at all times beneath the glow of a hot Middle Eastern sun. Prior to my departure I'd looked up the Kabul Serena hotel online. From what I could gather, it seemed like a nice place to stay, and there were a few locations around the hotel that would make for great scenery.

I fell into a deep sleep from which I awoke some hours later to the sounds of the attendants' voices. "Please put on your seat belts," they said.

I buckled my seat belt and peered about the plane. My fellow crew members were all awake. After buckling their seat belts, most of them returned to watching movies.

We landed at Charles de Gaulle Airport. Our private flight would not depart for four more hours, and the crew and I wasted a bit of time at a cafe near the airport. We sipped at some delicious coffee while waiting for our flight. Sitting in the cafe, we found that we couldn't understand anything that was being said around us save for the occasional 'bonjour'.

As we waited for our flight, I received a call from Mr. Sawyer. "How are you guys doing? I expect the flight to France went well?"

"It did," I said. "We're in Paris and we just have to wait a few hours for the next flight."

"Good, good. I hope you guys have a safe flight. Tell everyone I said hello."

The four hours sped by, and before we knew it we were boarding the private flight. As we approached the gate, the pilot came out to meet us. He introduced himself and we chatted briefly. He was stationed in France, but had a family who lived in New York. He led us to the plane, where we were shown to our seats.

The plane was quite different from the one we'd taken to France; it seemed more spacious. Perhaps this was due to the fact that the seats were each designed for only a single person. Without having to sit directly beside someone else, I found it easier to get comfortable and stretch out. The attendant rounded and made sure that we were all situated and told us that our equipment had been safely packed away in the storage area below.

As the plane took off, we were treated to a view of Paris. From so high up, it appeared a beautiful city. I was disappointed that I could not see more of it during my stay.

It wasn't long before the food came around. The menus were written in French, but also featured English translations. I ordered grilled chicken, steamed vegetables and, once more, a piece of baguette. As we ate, the attendant informed us that the flight would last for about eight hours. When I finished my meal, I leaned back in my seat to think about what was to come. The rest of the crew either slept or watched more movies.

I don't much recall the rest of the plane ride. I slept intermittently, catching sight of the time only once every few hours. The flight attendant tapped me on the shoulder and roused me from one such bout of sleep. "We'll be landing, sir. Please put on your seat belt."

I peered out of the window, getting my first glimpse of Kabul. Sure enough, the scenery was in line with what I'd imagined. Soaring over the ground, I saw distant mountains and small villages scattered about the land. The homes looked tiny from so high up, and the roads seemed surprisingly busy. Landing at the Kabul International Airport, I saw a small sign beside the runway that made me smile. "Welcome to Kabul," it read.

It occurred to me as we ambled out of the plane that the locals might not welcome Americans warmly. How would they react to my crew and I? I followed the rest of the crew off of the plane somewhat nervously. We gathered our belongings and began into the city.

5

Outside the airport, I spied a handful of parked buses and taxis. Gusts of hot wind rolled through the streets of Kabul. It was a dry heat, quite unlike the summer humidity with which I was accustomed in Detroit. We'd made our way through the airport with ease. Unlike the others I'd visited recently, the Kabul International Airport was surprisingly quiet. Looking at the list of departures and arrivals, I found their schedule rather scarce. Only a small number of planes would be landing over the course of the day to come.

The rest of the crew marched along as though they were in an American airport. Having been there before, it seemed that their surroundings didn't surprise them in the least. I picked up my bags at the baggage claim and the rest of the crew began the slow process of retrieving the equipment.

At the baggage claim, one of the airline employees brought Max to us in his carrier. The poor dog looked rather tired. The flight had probably taken a lot out of him. I took the carrier in hand and peeked inside. "How's it going, Max?" I asked.

He perked up immediately and began barking.

"We'll let you out of there just as soon as we make it to the hotel," I said. When all of the cases were accounted for, we began for the exit.

"Here, let me take those bags," said Ruth. She plucked the bags from my hand and set them on a cart.

"Are you sure?" I asked. "It's no trouble. I can carry them."

She simply smiled and shook her head. Although I was thankful, I felt a little bad making her take my things. Having a personal assistant would take some getting used to.

Ruth was a quiet woman. Although she spoke very little however, I could sense a great discipline about her. She communicated it through her actions, displaying reliability and calm. When she did speak, she was careful to choose her words, relaying only exactly what she wished to convey. This delicate manner of hers was important; she'd handled numerous calls on the way to Kabul with the folks back at RBC headquarters in New York.

Leaving the airport, we found a large truck waiting for us. The driver welcomed us in Pashto and helped us load up our bags. I thanked him in kind, which made him take pause. "Your Pashto is quite good," he said with a chuckle. I laughed; it was hard to say how many times the locals would tell me that during my time in Kabul. I certainly didn't look like the sort of person who'd be proficient in Pashto. My speaking abilities were sure to surprise many others throughout the course of this job.

When all of us were seated, we began for the hotel. It proved only a short distance from the airport, which allowed me only a brief glance at the streets of Kabul. The driver made haste; parking beside the hotel's entrance and helping us unload our things. Several hotel employees came out to welcome us and help us with our luggage. Several of them attempted to greet us in English; however the tones of their native tongue overlapped those of English and made their greetings rather hard to understand. I smiled and thanked them as they took my bags from Ruth and carried them into the lobby. I took up Max's carrier and started inside.

In the lobby a small group of locals looked upon us with a certain awe. Certainly they weren't used to seeing so many foreigners at once. Nonetheless, they said nothing to us as we passed. One of the hotel employees came up to me as we entered.

"I'm sorry, sir. We don't allow pets," he said to me.

"Oh, I see." I wasn't sure what to do. Max had made the flight all the way here. What would I do with him if he couldn't stay at the hotel?

"It's no problem," said Ruth, taking the carrier. "I'll handle it."

I thanked her and we began through the lobby towards the elevator, where we all squeezed in and rose to the second floor.

The employees showed us each to our rooms. We were each assigned our own rooms along the same hall. At the end of the hall were my quarters which,

thanks to the stipulations in my contract, were a suite.
I thanked the employee and carried my bags into the
suite. It was a massive room, featuring a bedroom
space, a bathroom, a living room and kitchen.

I was packing away my clothes in a chest of
drawers when I heard an uproar outside my window.
Curious, I set aside my things and peered outside.
Two young men stood below, yelling at each other with
ferocity. I listened closely, but soon realized my inability
to understand their vernacular. I'd been taught only
proper Pashto. As a result, it would take me some time
to understand the common slang in the area. Still, I
listened to their argument.

One of the men appeared to be an employee
at a local market, whereas the other was a customer.
From what I could gather, the customer was angry
at the employee because he'd been overcharged at
the market. A third gentleman came towards them to
seemingly calm them down as they screamed through
the streets.

I returned to my chores, putting away clothes

and supplies, and wondering whether I'd be safe walking through the city. There was no telling how the locals would react to me-- especially if they knew that I spoke Pashto. Furthermore, I wasn't nearly as comfortable here as the rest of the crew was. The locals could probably sense that.

I heard a knock at my door and found Ruth waiting for me in the hall. "How are you doing? Do you need help with anything?" she asked.

"No, I think I'm alright. I'm nearly done. What's up?"

"Well, I just wanted to let you know that tomorrow's story has been cancelled. The rundown for the evening show is full, so we're just going to collect footage of the streets so that the anchors back home can do a quick story."

I was disappointed, but looked forward to using the free time to explore the city. "I see. Thanks for letting me know. I'll see you tomorrow, then?"

"Bright and early," she replied. "Oh, and one

more thing."

"Yeah?"

"I spoke to the guys back home at RBC headquarters. They've arranged for Max to stay in an outdoor area. It's just outside the hotel, so you'll be able to see him whenever you like."

"Hey, thanks Ruth!" I said. "I appreciate that. Hopefully the heat isn't too much for him. I know I'm not used to it yet."

"I'm sure he'll be fine," she assured me as she began down the hall to her own room.

I returned to my quarters and, feeling somewhat jet-lagged, decided to get some rest.

***

I awoke at nine in the morning, feeling well-rested. For whatever reason, I never had too much trouble adjusting to time-changes. With more than nine hours of sleep, I felt prepared to take on my first full day in Afghanistan. I heard another knock at my door just as

I finished showering.

It was Ruth. "Hey, I was just making sure you were awake. Did you sleep alright?"

"Yeah," I said. "I slept great. And you?"

"Like a baby. When you're done getting ready, meet us downstairs for breakfast."

"Sure thing," I said. I finished getting dressed and made my way to the hotel lobby for a quick breakfast.

The rest of the crew was waiting for me when I arrived. It seemed they were all early-risers. I'd been the only one to sleep in till nine and felt a bit embarrassed as a result. While we ate, various other English-speaking journalists came up to us and introduced themselves. As the folks at RBC headquarters had told me, the Kabul Serena Hotel was the hotel of choice for foreign journalists covering the news in Kabul.

One of the journalists, Chris, was a fellow American. He didn't work for an American news station however; he'd been employed by a large station in the U.K. He'd been sent to Afghanistan to cover the war, much like I had been. He wasn't nearly as skilled in Pashto as I was however, and had only begun to learn the language upon his arrival. We talked about a great and many things over breakfast, and I found myself impressed with his Pashto. For only having begun to learn it, he seemed to be doing quite well.

Michael came up to Chris and I as we conversed. Apparently, they'd met during a previous trip to Afghanistan, where Michael had been working with another journalist. Chris told us a story about how he'd recently taped a story in a rather dangerous area. "We'd scouted out the area in advance and felt pretty safe about it. All of a sudden though, we began picking up a lot of gunfire. We were taping at the time and all of us just froze up for a while. It was terrifying-- scariest thing I've had happen to me yet while reporting abroad."

"I'll bet," I replied. "That sounds pretty frightening. Is that the only time you've ever come across such a thing?"

"It is, yeah. So far at least."

I couldn't necessarily say that I was scared to

walk the streets of Kabul, however there did exist in my heart a persistent apprehension. I trusted the members of my crew and felt that their experience would help keep me safe, however I couldn't help but wonder if, like Chris, we'd end up in potentially dangerous areas. How would we react? Would we be able to protect ourselves? On the news back home, I'd always heard a lot about the sacrifice of our troops overseas. Certainly our troops on the front lines faced extraordinary danger. That danger wasn't simply reserved for members of the armed forces however. Civilians and journalists like myself were also at risk. What sort of sacrifices would I have to make, I wondered.

Chris had sacrificed many things in taking this job. Upon leaving the U.S. for the U.K., he'd been forced to leave behind his family. Although overseas, the U.K. proved similar enough to the U.S. But upon leaving the U.K. for Afghanistan, he'd left behind every shred of normalcy. Suddenly, he was in a much more unfamiliar place where a completely different language was spoken and a radically different culture dominated. He asserted that the sacrifice had been great, but that the job had its rewards also. He felt more mature than he had in the United States, and said that he'd learned much more about the world around him through his travels.

It was 11 AM by the time we finished our breakfast. I found myself enjoying the leisurely pace of the morning. In Detroit, I'd have been forced to stick to a strict deadline. Here however, with only a few simple shots to capture, I found myself feeling liberated. The crew and I gathered up our things and left the hotel.

A dusty wind ran through the streets of Kabul as we emerged. I eyed my surroundings as I crossed the threshold, taking in the sights with wonder. The first thing I noticed were the passers-by. Nearly all of them were men. From time to time I'd see a woman pass by with her husband and children, however they proved surprisingly scarce. The sun was high and bright that afternoon, and I found myself rather uncomfortable due to the heat.

I followed the crew through the crowded streets for nearly half a mile. It was at that time that we came upon a small U.S. Military base. At the gate we were welcomed by a group of soldiers and were admitted into the base to talk. I couldn't help but jump as we entered the base. In the distance I could see the peaks of several mountains from which there rang out numerous gunshots. I looked about me at the rest of the crew, however they all appeared relaxed. It was as though they couldn't hear the shots ringing in the distance.

In the base, one of the soldiers came up to me. "Wait a minute-- you're Stephen, aren't you? Stephen Cook?" He laughed heartily and shook my hand. "You're never gonna believe this, but I used to watch you on the news with my family all the time!" The soldier introduced himself as Brian, a citizen of Detroit such as myself. His family still lived in Detroit, in an apartment complex not too far from the one I had lived in. "Small, small world," he laughed. "It seems like just yesterday I was watching you on the evening news."

"Thanks," I said. I was flattered that he'd recognized me and at how excited he was to meet me. Perhaps my presence reminded him somewhat of his family waiting back in Detroit. It felt good to be acknowledged for my work, as well as to bring someone comfort.

I respected the soldiers at the base. Like Brian, many of them had left behind families to fight the war, and many of them had sacrificed their lives. Watching the news coverage in the United States, it was easy to forget just how many of our men and women were serving abroad. Seeing them in action and relying on them for protection reminded me of just how thankful I was for their service.

We captured a bit of footage around the base and then visited a nearby restaurant. We picked up a few sandwiches to-go and continued through the streets. We nibbled on our sandwiches and took more footage as we headed back to the hotel. The oppressive heat proved hard to bear. I wasn't sure whether I could ever get used to such powerful, relentless heat.

Upon arriving at the hotel, we set to editing the footage we'd taken and forwarded it to the directors back at RBC headquarters in New York. They sent us a response upon receiving it and asked us to gather more footage. Michael and William hiked out with the gear to a small mountain a few miles from the hotel. From there, they captured a panoramic shot of Kabul and surrounding areas.

It was after 6 PM by the time we were done. With all of the footage sent, we decided to seek out dinner. I could see why journalists enjoyed staying at the Kabul Serena Hotel; it was conveniently located astride numerous fine restaurants and shops. The crew and I began through the streets in search of a place to dine and decided upon a small restaurant in an alley behind the hotel. Chairs and tables had been set up outside, however the heat made it too hot to eat there.

"I'm sorry, but I was wondering. Do you folks have air conditioning inside?" I asked one of the employees in broken Pashto.

"No, I'm afraid not," he replied.

We continued walking and decided upon a larger restaurant further down the street. The front entrance of the place was being remodeled, and we were corralled along to the side of the building as a result. It was explained to me that the remodeling was due to damage incurred by a small bombing that had occurred some months earlier. Apparently, a bomb had been planted on the building which caused great damage and injured four employees.

Walking in through the back entrance, I was delighted to feel a stream of cold air. The manager welcomed us warmly and seated us. He returned a short while later with samples of various dishes. "I wonder," I asked him, "can we sit closer to the front. I'd like to get a look at the damage there, if possible."

We switched tables. "Were you here when this happened?" I asked the manager.

"I was, yes. I was preparing to open for the day when the bomb went off. I ended up with a broken arm, but it could have been worse," he said.

From behind the counter he pulled out a series of photos he'd taken of the damage. The amount of damage caused by a single bomb proved astonishing. I thanked him and took a seat with the rest of the crew.

We ordered Palao; a rice dish with meat and

vegetables piled on top. We also ordered kabobs and Bonjan salad. Overall, the food was delicious, however I found my appetite stifled somewhat by the heat. I ate a decent amount and thanked the owner again for his hospitality. He took good care of us and seemed friendly towards Americans.

Despite the damage and loss, I thought it inspiring that the restaurant owner was repairing his building. The blast had been devastating to the building and to those who worked within, however in a display of true strength, the owner had set to rebuilding things. It was inspirational to me. He might have chosen to sulk in fear, but instead of displaying weakness, he worked hard to re-establish his business in the face of danger.

I was set to do a segment for the 6 PM news in the States, and would have to stay up till about 3 AM as a result. I asked Glenda to take some footage of the restaurant and their reconstruction efforts before returning to the hotel. The crew and I lazed in the hotel lobby till nearly 10 PM.

At 10, we decided to begin preparing for our

segment. We trekked to a small mountain behind the hotel and set up our gear. Lighting, audio, satellites, cables, cameras, teleprompters, computers and production team were all in sync, working in tandem to create as professional a broadcast as possible. The shot would only last about two minutes, however we couldn't afford to cut any corners. Working for a national station, there was no telling how many Americans would be watching our broadcast.

I prepared for the story by reviewing the video and preparing my voiceover. The story was about the current atmosphere in Afghanistan. I was asked to report upon the current tensions, the politics in the region, troop activity and the war's future. I decided to add in a few seconds of footage that Glenda had taken at the restaurant to the story as David and Michael busied themselves with editing.

The broadcast went well and, when it was finished, we went about packing up all of our gear.

"I'll be seeing you guys tomorrow morning in the lobby," said William as we began for the hotel.

"We'll see about our next story in the morning. I'll be sure to give you a full briefing concerning the details, Stephen," said Ruth.

I thanked them and wished them all a good night as they continued to the hotel. I decided to stop by the outdoor area where Max was staying. I wanted to see him for a while before heading off to bed.

I arrived at the pet area, which was cordoned off by a large fence. I opened the gate and entered, which sent Max into frenzy.

"Aw, how's it going, boy? Did you miss me?" I asked.

Max rolled on the ground as I pat his belly. "Things sure are different out here, aren't they? It's a completely different world. And to think we were in Detroit just a short while ago."

I looked up at the moon. That moon and the dog at my feet were the only familiar things in sight.

6

My time in Afghanistan was off to a great start. Within my first few weeks, I was called upon to report on diverse subjects which brought me into contact with local leaders, American soldiers, militants and numerous of Kabul's locals. As time went on, my Pashto improved and I began to feel more comfortable about using it with the locals. I caught on to their slang and very soon felt as though I could communicate with them on a nearly even level. I still couldn't get used to the heat, but had learned to dress in cooler clothing to somewhat offset its effects.

The folks at RBC headquarters seemed to be very pleased with our work. Although we didn't work with the rigid structure I was used to in Detroit, we still managed to carry out our work with great efficiency. We would meet each day in the hotel lobby, where Ruth would give us a daily briefing. We'd discuss current news in the U.S. before delving into the stories we'd have to cover for the day. It didn't take me long to get into this rhythm and I found that I enjoyed working this way.

On some days, the folks at RBC headquarters would have no story requests. On those days we'd often relax or sightsee, capturing footage along the way that we could later use in our reports. In the process, I came to know the members of my crew more intimately, and began to form strong friendships with each of them. There were also a few chaotic incidents along the way.

From time to time, we'd receive word about breaking news. When such stories broke, no matter the time, the crew would dash out of the hotel, sometimes still in pajamas, to cover the story as quickly as possible. There had been a few instances during my first weeks where we'd been awoken from a dead sleep to cover intense battles or bombings. RBC had provided us with a large van to use, and on those nights, we'd loaded our gear hastily into the back before speeding off to the site of the story.

I recall on one such night, William awoke each of us frantically. "Wake up, Stephen," he told me. "We've got some serious military activity going on just past the mountains. We've got to get out there fast."

Half asleep, I'd thrown on a t-shirt and a pair of sandals and lurched into the hall, where various of my fellow crew members had also assembled. As we left the hotel, hauling cases of gear, we could hear the sounds of gunfire in the distance. Michael took the wheel and sped from the hotel to a small side-street. "We'll be there in about ten minutes," he said. "Can you guys get things ready in that time?"

Glenda and Daniel nodded and began to hurriedly set up some of the gear. They switched on cameras, held quick tests for audio and video and talked about the optimal positioning for each device.

"You should probably decide what you're going to say," Ruth said to me. She handed me a piece of paper and a pen.

"Alright, William. What's up, exactly?" I asked.

William filled me in on the details. At some point in the night, a bomb reportedly went off somewhere near the mountains. The explosion had been followed by persistent and heavy gunfire. William had received intel and had been monitoring the area for a few hours.

Upon receiving word of the blast, he'd awoken all of us. "Things have escalated, so this is news-worthy. There's no telling what's going on over there, so we need to be cautious. I'll scout out the area and we'll shoot from a safe location. No venturing outside of the safety-zone, got that?"

I nodded and began drafting content. Despite the inherent danger, there was a certain thrill to this kind of journalism. We were doing things spontaneously, leaning on the hard-won expertise of the crew to create a high-quality broadcast. This was what journalism was all about.

We arrived in the area and William quickly set to defining the safety-zone. The others began to set up the equipment as Ruth and I went over my part. When everything was set, the cameras did a pan of the area and settled upon me.

"Hello, this is Stephen Cook, reporting from Kabul, Afghanistan. We've received word from various sources that there have been explosions in this area as well as prolonged gunfire. The combatants and the nature of the conflict are not yet clear; however we'll be sure to fill you in as the details become available."

The smell of gunpowder tickled my nostrils. The sounds of war were closer now than they'd ever been, and as I spoke to the camera, I found myself stifling a shiver. My veins were coursing with adrenaline. During a break, I looked over at William, who was diligently monitoring the situation. Our lives were in his hands.

When the story was complete, we piled quickly into the van and fled to the hotel. We received a call shortly thereafter from the guys at RBC headquarters, congratulating us. "Fine work, guys. Is everyone all right?"

Safe and sound in the hotel, we all had a good laugh. It's a common coping strategy for those who have faced great stress, and each and every one of us, no matter how seasoned, laughed heartily. We stayed up a brief while longer and, when William gave us the go-ahead, returned to our rooms.

Another day, the folks at RBC had requested that we report upon the local atmosphere. I chose to do a story on the restaurant near the hotel, which had been damaged heavily by a bomb. I interviewed the owner and translated his story for the American people, and the broadcast, I was told, had been quite a success Stateside. I'd worked hard to provide an accurate portrait of the current tensions in Kabul, but wanted to feature the courage of its citizens all the while.

"The owner of this restaurant in Kabul was hospitalized with a broken arm some time ago due to the blast that wrecked the entrance to his restaurant," I said during the report. Pointing to the damaged areas, I continued. "As you can see, the damage was extensive. Nonetheless, the owner of this shop has worked tirelessly to re-build. He refuses to be intimidated by the chaos that has enveloped the region, and his example provides strength to those around him."

The thankful owner gave a tearful account of the events, which I translated for American viewers. In the days to come, he offered us many free meals.

Before I realized it, my first month in Afghanistan had passed. We'd covered numerous stories and met many incredible people. It was around this time that I finally began to feel comfortable in my new position. The crew and I got along like old friends and had fine-tuned our respective tasks to the point where we could literally shoot a story given only a moment's notice.

We'd done another piece, interviewing soldiers at the U.S. base. The soldiers, many of whom were homesick, seemed to appreciate the opportunity to be interviewed. Throughout the course of the story, I interviewed several soldiers, including Brian. They relayed their continued dedication to the war effort and expressed interest in returning to their families as soon as possible. It felt good to provide an outlet for the war-weary soldiers.

On a Sunday, when RBC hadn't given us anything to report on, I'd been approached by Ruth. "I've got a call for you, Stephen," she said.

"Hello?" I said, taking her mobile phone.

"Stephen?" I could tell; it was my mother.

"Mom? Hey, how are you? It's great to hear your

voice!"

"I'm fine, Stephen. How are you sweetheart? Is everything OK? We've been watching you on the news. You seem to be doing well. You've been doing a great job."

"Thanks mom, I appreciate that. "How've you guys been?"

"Oh, you know. Same as always, Stephen. We've been worried about you, of course. Are you staying safe? Please be careful," she said.

"Yeah, mom, everything's been good. I've got a security advisor working on my crew and the other members have all been here before. I was nervous at first, but honestly I've gotten used to things around here. It's not as bad as it sounds on the news. It's true that there are bombings and gunfights, but for the most part, the city is safe."

"That's good," she replied. "Oh, here's your dad."

"Hello," said my dad. "How are you doing Stephen?"

"I'm good, dad. How are you?"

"Fine, fine," he said. "You've been doing great work on the news. We make sure to watch RBC's broadcasts every day to see if we can catch your segments. I'm proud of you."

"Thanks, dad."

"Oh, and you did a great job with that translation during your segment with the restaurant owner. I can see why they chose you, my boy. You've certainly got your work down pat," he said. "Just promise me you'll stay safe. I keep telling your mother that you're a smart kid, that you've got a good head on your shoulders, but you know how she worries. Don't make me look like a liar now," he laughed.

"I won't, dad. I'll do my best to stay safe. I can't wait to see you guys again! It'll be a while, but I'm sure I'll have some great stories for you by the time I get back."

"I look forward to it," he said.

"Well, I've got to get going, dad. Thanks for

calling, though. Tell mom I said goodbye."

"I will. Take care, Stephen."

The folks at RBC headquarters had forwarded the call to Ruth's phone. I called them back and thanked them for their trouble.

The remainder of the day was spent sightseeing. I'd visited some wonderful places around Kabul. My favorite spot was in the mountains near the hotel. When there was nothing in the way of fighting going on, I enjoyed trekking to the base of the mountains and looking out upon Kabul. Perhaps it was merely the crosswinds that existed there due to the higher elevation, however the mountains seemed cooler to me than the city, which made for a relaxing change of pace. I spent many afternoons hiking about the mountains with members of my crew. We'd amassed a great deal of footage from the area and had even used some of it in our broadcasts.

***

In his usual fashion, William knocked on my door. Three solid taps. I knew it was him and what he had to tell me before I even opened the door.

"Do you hear that?" he asked. He was referring to the sound of bombs that had been filling the air for a few minutes prior.

"I do, yeah," I replied.

"The guys at RBC are still getting back to me. I think they're going to want to dispatch a group to cover the fight, but I'm not sure exactly what kind of shot they're looking for. I'll keep you posted, but stay close to the hotel, in case this develops into something more serious."

"Will do," I said. "I'm just going to step outside to get some air. If you need me, I'll be hanging out with Max in the outdoor area."

"Alright," he said.

I left the hotel and entered the fenced area where Max was happily jumping about. The dog ran up to me excitedly, as though he hadn't seen me in ages. I was scarcely able to scratch behind his ears and play a little fetch with him before William's voice drifted through the air from a window on the upper story of the hotel. "Stephen, get in here, man. We're going to have to get going."

As I left to meet up with the others, Max's relentless barking echoed against the buildings. "It's alright, boy," I said as I was leaving. "I'll see you soon." Nonetheless, his barking would not cease.

I returned to the hotel, where the crew was waiting solemnly. "It looks like several U.S. Soldiers have died out there, Stephen. There's a huge firefight going on, and we're not sure at this moment who's winning. The guys at headquarters want us to cover it," said Ruth. "It's going to be a dangerous job, it seems. We're going to have to be extra careful to stay hidden. The last thing we'd want is for our reporting to attract the attention of violent militants."

"Alright," I said. "Is everyone ready? When do we head out?"

William shook his head. "Seeing as this is such a

dangerous job, it wouldn't make a whole lot of sense for us to send our whole crew out there, Stephen. Moving in large numbers will only slow us down and it could attract attention to us. I've been advised by the guys at headquarters to send only three of you. You, Daniel and a photographer." He looked over at Michael and Glenda. "Which one of you is it going to be?"

They looked at each other, as though they couldn't decide. It was the first time I'd ever seen either of them displaying anything like anxiety. Up till that point, they'd been stalwart and fearless. To see them so indecisive made me more than a little nervous. If they were afraid to take on this job, then how would I fare so close to the battlefield?

"OK, which of the photographers is coming with me?" I asked.

"I'll come along," said Michael with a sigh. "I haven't shot a story like this one in a while."

The three of us prepared our gear. We loaded up only a simple assortment of devices; cameras, a soundboard and a few others. Daniel carried it all into the van while I spoke to William.

"I'll be monitoring the situation closely. Listen through your IFB for instructions. If things get dangerous, I'm going to pull you guys out of there. Got that?" said William.

I put in my earpiece. "Sounds good. Keep an eye on things out there for us," I said.

"I will. Good luck. Come back in one piece, alright guys? Keep your wits about you. Things can get frightening out there, but just stick to my instructions and everything should be alright."

The crew wished us luck. Daniel, Michael and I piled into the van and took off for the mountains, uncertain of what we'd find there.

As we drove along, the three of us couldn't help but express our nervousness. The intensity of the fighting was unlike anything I'd yet witnessed. Occasionally an explosion would sound, which would shake the ground for a brief time. Considering how far away the battle was taking place, it was clear that the bombs being used were powerful.

"The gunfire's not letting up," said Michael as he fiddled nervously with the camera. "This is going to be a pretty big fight, I imagine. You guys ready?"

I shook my head. "Haven't got a choice. Have you covered fights like this one before?" I asked my companions.

"Once or twice, yeah," replied Daniel. "I've never had a problem; we just need to do our job and get out of there before things escalate any further. If we're careless, we could put ourselves in serious danger. Heck, even if we're careful, we could end up in danger. That's the nature of the beast, I'm afraid."

"Has anyone ever been seriously hurt during any of those stories?" I asked. I almost didn't want to hear the answer.

"No, knock on wood. We've been lucky. In some ways, that's all you've got out here; luck. Don't worry, Stephen. I know how you feel. We'll be alright, though."

Daniel pressed hard on the accelerator, which

left a massive cloud of dust in our wake. "At any rate, we need to hurry. Our guys are dying out there. The people back in the States need to know about this."

I spied a frightening determination in his eyes as he drove towards the mountains. Daniel's focus was contagious. I took pause, considering what I'd say during the report. There were many people in the States whose loved ones were fighting this war. To do any less than professional work would be to slight them. I rehearsed in my head as we drove along.

Michael conducted a video test and recorded some test footage to make certain that the sound settings were correct. He hummed a song to himself as he worked. It was clear that he was quite nervous as well.

We drove on for a brief while. Before long, the mountains came into clear view. "It looks like we've arrived," said Michael, throwing the camera up onto his shoulder. "It's showtime, folks."

Daniel parked the car hastily and dragged a knotted mass of equipment out onto the ground.

Through my IFB, William gave us directions.

"Over there, near that ridge, you'll want to report from there. It's a good spot for cover. Keep your eyes open. Be aware of your surroundings. I'll be looking out for you guys as well."

"Alright, will do." I positioned myself by the ridge and recited a few lines in my head. I'd introduce myself and then briefly touch upon the details of the battle as William made them available.

The fragrant smell of gunpowder drifted through the air. Smoke and dust rose up to obscure the orange sun as we prepared to shoot. Echoing against the mountains, the constant pounding of machine guns seemed almost too hard to bear. My ears were ringing; it was all I could do to focus on the voices coming through my IFB.

"Alright, Stephen. Ready when you are," said Michael, hoisting the camera into position.

I nodded and the broadcast promptly began.

"What's it like out there, Mr. Cook?" I heard one

of the anchors ask through my IFB. "It sounds as though there's a lot of action going on out there."

"Well, as you can see, there's a good bit of smoke in the distance. Several bombs have detonated over the past few minutes alone, and the sound of shelling is ubiquitous. I've received word that several U.S. Soldiers have been killed during this exchange, however details are forthcoming. We'll be sure to keep you folks posted."

A short while later, the same anchor asked me through my earpiece if there'd been any developments. A blast shook the ground from nearby, and I stumbled somewhat. "The blasts seem to be getting closer-- as you can probably see. The fighting is intense, and there has been no decrease in shelling since last we spoke."

" I do hope you and your crew are staying safe amid this fighting," said one of the anchors.

"We're doing our best," I said to the camera with a nod. "Let me see if I can't find a better angle. I'd like for our viewers to get a better look at what's really going on out here."

I climbed up on the ridge a bit, to get a better view of the fight. Michael followed close behind, capturing a massive plume of smoke that rose into the air from a freshly-detonated bomb.

"Be careful, Stephen. That's risky," I heard William say through my earpiece.

"What is it we're seeing out there, Mr. Cook?" asked the anchor.

I scanned the distance, but could make out only vague details due to the smoke and dust that circulated about the battlefield. "It's too hard to say at this moment. We'll have to let the smoke clear first," I said. "It appears that the fighting continues, although I'm not sure exactly who it is we're seeing directly ahead of us."

Michael nudged me on the shoulder. "What is that, Stephen?" he asked, pointing just over the ridge.

"What?" I asked, peering towards the side of the mountain.

"Stephen, get out of--"

William's words were cut off by a sudden, tremendous blast. A wave of dust and rocks blossomed all about us, knocking us aside as though we were rag dolls. Michael lost his grip on the camera, and it tumbled a great distance. The sudden burst of dust and rocks was soon followed by a wave of intense heat. A blinding white light overcame my vision as I was thrust back against the side of the mountain. The last thing I can recall before losing consciousness, is hearing William in my earpiece.

"Stephen? Stephen?"

7

Admittedly, my memory of the events directly following the bombing in the mountains is murky. I was filled in by the members of the crew about what transpired after the blast, and it is only through their testimony that I've been able to fill in the blanks and understand what went on in the time before I awoke in the hospital.

I was surprised to find myself at the Cleveland Clinic when I awoke. Unconscious for so long, my mind had still occupied Kabul. Upon opening my eyes and registering the sights, I thought myself dreaming initially. I found myself in a hospital bed, unable to move and accosted by a tremendous pain. Shortly after I awoke, a nurse entered the room.

"Oh my goodness, you're awake, Mr. Cook," she said, setting aside a handful of medications. "Let me go get the doctor!"

She ran from the room and called out for a doctor. She returned a short while later with a stern-looking man in a white lab coat. They closed the door behind them and the doctor set immediately to examining me. When he was through, he took a seat on a stool at my side. "How are you feeling, Mr. Cook?"

I couldn't seem to answer. I tried to speak, however some aspect of my body could not seem to facilitate speech. Had my throat been damaged in the blast? What was the matter with me?

The doctor sighed and examined me once more. "You've been through a lot, Mr. Cook. I imagine that you're quite confused at the moment, however I'd like to shed some light on a few things if I may. First of all, can you understand me?"

I tried to nod, but found myself unable to move.

"If you can understand me, blink twice," he said.

I blinked twice. It was all I could do to communicate with him, it seemed.

He nodded. "Good. Your mind is intact, it seems." He stood and paced about a bit. "Mr. Cook, you were reporting in the mountains near Kabul, Afghanistan when a bomb detonated near you and your crew. It was a powerful blast; you're lucky to have survived."

I listened intently to what he had to say.

"You're at the Cleveland Clinic, in Ohio," he continued. "We're taking good care of you here, however the extent of your injuries is not yet known. We're monitoring you closely, and will fill you in on your prognosis as soon as we can. How is your pain, Mr. Cook? Please blink twice if it is intense."

I blinked twice. My senses were inflamed with an all-encompassing ache. It felt as though I'd been hit by a truck.

"I see. Well, that's to be expected. I'll have the nurse here administer some pain medication. It's all we can do for you at the moment until we learn the full extent of your injuries. I ask that you try your best to rest, Mr. Cook. You'll likely have some difficult days ahead and you'll also have some difficult decisions to make about your future. Please do your best to rest for the time being and we'll see what we can do to better facilitate you," he said. He then told the nurse to administer a pain medication.

I wasn't sure what he meant. What sort of damage had I sustained? What sort of decisions would I have to make? I was unable to move; why was this? Had I been paralyzed by the blast? Would I recover fully, or was my body ruined? Rather than comfort, his words filled me with dread.

Another nurse entered my room a brief while later with an IV bag full of pain medication. As the medication took effect, I found myself becoming terribly drowsy. I drifted off into an uneasy sleep, my mind filled only with visions of Afghanistan. I dreamt of gunpowder and earth-shaking blasts. I dreamt about my crew as well.

The next few days were marked by longer periods of lucidity. I was still unconscious most of the time, but managed to awaken at least once a day to listen to the doctors or nurses as they spoke to me. Still, I found myself unable to speak. It was rather strange and frightening to be relegated to silence in such a way. The doctor avoided discussing the extent of my injuries, probably because he didn't want me to worry while incapacitated. In retrospect, I'm glad he did so.

The pain never fully abated. No matter the medications I was given, I could not totally ignore the pain that surged through me. The nurses did their best to keep me comfortable, administering medications on a rigid schedule. Nonetheless, their efforts could only relieve me so much. The bulk of the time I spent conscious was spent in great suffering. When my body didn't ail me, I found it was my mind which convulsed incessantly with a new and terrible fear. How long had I been in the hospital? How much longer would I have to stay? Would I ever recover? Worse than being confined to the hospital with unknown injuries was being unable to communicate my fears.

Each day the doctor would come in to assess me. He would ask me to blink twice to answer various of his questions. "How is your pain today," he would ask. "Have you been sleeping well?" I would blink once to reply in the negative, twice in the affirmative. He would watch closely for my response and then nod accordingly, logging my answers on a clipboard and making decisions based on them. "I think we're close to understanding the extent of your injuries. We'll be

going over many things with you in the days to come,
Mr. Cook. I ask that you stay strong and keep an open
mind as we do so. You may not like what you hear, but
I assure you that my staff and I will be here to help you
every step of the way. You can rely on us as you seek to
become healthy again."

Keep an open mind. The folks at RBC
headquarters had asked me to do the same thing when
reading about my new position. Had I been able to
laugh, I'd have done so heartily. It was surreal, being
confined to the bed for so long. By the sound of it, my
injuries were life-altering. The doctor seemed to think
that I was going to live, which was good news, however I
wasn't sure how the blast would compromise my quality
of life. Would I remain paralyzed? Would I be disfigured
in some way? Somehow, the advice of *keep an open
mind* didn't bode well at the time.

***

It was on an afternoon, I believe, that the doctor
came to discuss my injuries. He went through his usual
routine, asking me a number of questions about my

comfort, before taking a seat at the stool and rubbing at his temples. Before he'd even begun to speak I realized the subject he was preparing to broach. He seemed to have trouble finding the words, and spent a great deal of time searching for them at my bedside. Finally, he began.

"Mr. Cook," he said, "I believe it's time for me to tell you what it is you're in the hospital for. Admittedly, I didn't want to tell you too soon for fear that you might react badly to the news. To be quite honest, you're in quite poor shape, and for a while my colleagues and I weren't sure whether or not you'd make it. Seeing as you've pulled through, I think it important to fill you in now on the extent of your injuries, as well as to your options for treatment.

"You were brought here in a terrible state-- transferred from a small hospital somewhere in Kabul. They didn't have the facilities to care for you, and it appears that the staff at RBC arranged for you to be transported to the United States along with a group of returning soldiers. When they brought you here, we ran a gamut of tests. We knew you were alive, but little else.

"Medicine is an imperfect science; a lot of what we do here is, for lack of a better word, guess-work. We knew that you were alive, and yet the extent of your injuries was so great, we were uncertain where to start in your treatment. We ran several radiological exams, as well as tests for infection. Your wounds were terrible, and we did what we could to cleanse and dress them.

"Recently," he continued, "I've been able to discuss the findings of a CT scan we performed on your brain with a skilled radiologist. There was a bit of encephalopathy, however it seems that the swelling has gone down and you're out of the woods in that regard. It's a good thing, too. Had your brain continued to swell, there's no telling whether you'd have survived. The rest of your injuries however, are something of a mixed bag, Mr. Cook."

I could see him growing nervous. He seemed a good man, the sort who cared little for delivering bad news to his patients. Although he was bringing me bad news, I found myself feeling a bit bad for him instead.

"Do you understand everything I've told you so

far, Mr. Cook?" he asked. "Blink twice if so."

I blinked twice and he continued.

"Your brain is free of damage. Some of your major organs were bruised, but seem to be healing nicely. I'm afraid however, that your limbs were lost in the blast. Both arms and both legs were severed in the blast, it seems, and in the past weeks we've set to cleaning and sealing off those wounds."

My mind spiraled at once into despair. I wanted to cry out, but found myself unable. My eyes welled with tears as the doctor asked me to blink twice for him. He saw the look in my eye and became conciliatory, however there was little he could say at that moment to make me feel better.

It was little wonder I was unable to move. I'd been confined to the bed, paralyzed and wreaked with tremendous pain due to the severing of my limbs. It all made sense now. I wasn't sure how to feel at that time, and it was all I could do to choke back tears.

"I understand that this is a very difficult time for

you, Mr. Cook. I'm sorry to have delivered such terrible news unto you. You've suffered greatly and I know that news of this kind is not at all conducive to your comfort. Nonetheless, you're alive. If nothing else, you should be thankful for that."

What would become of my career? I'd finally been promoted, working a dream job for a national station. How was I to continue? Had my dreams really been brought to a halt so suddenly?

"The team here is committed to helping you recuperate, Stephen. It will be difficult, no doubt, however there are numerous options for therapy and rehabilitation. Although your quality of life will be impacted in some ways due to these injuries, I feel confident that we can help you live a fulfilling life to some degree. So long as you choose to pursue rehabilitation with enthusiasm, anything is possible. I apologize once more for having brought you such bad news today. I'll be back tomorrow to discuss possible treatments with you."

The doctor stood up to leave. "Oh, and Mr. Cook. I assume you're somewhat curious about what transpired in Afghanistan, and about your crew. I've contacted RBC headquarters in New York, and they'll be sending a representative to discuss these matters with you. They should be arriving by this evening. I've given them your room number; you can expect to see them within a few hours."

With that, the doctor walked out, his head hanging low.

***

Time seemed to pass quite slowly as I waited for the RBC representative. Despite the promise of rehabilitation, I could not shake the dread I felt. I wondered if I'd ever be able to live in a satisfying fashion again; if I'd ever be able to speak, or if I'd remain an invalid. The prospect frightened me to no end. I was used to autonomy. I'd lived an active, fast-paced lifestyle and worked very hard over the years to further my career. And for what? What would happen to it all now?

The light drifting in through the blinds transitioned from a powdery white to a light orange as the sun began to set. The nurse came in every few hours to administer various medications and to make sure I was comfortable. I felt numb however, still shell-shocked by the sudden news.

It was just after the sun had set that I heard a knock at the door. I peered over and, to my surprise, Ruth walked in. She ambled over to my bed slowly, her expression rather pensive and pallid. "Hello, Stephen," she said quietly.

She took a seat beside my bed and looked into my eyes. "Oh thank goodness," she said. "You're finally awake. We weren't sure that you'd ever wake up."

It was nice to see Ruth. For a moment I forgot all about my injuries and felt at ease. While relieved, she seemed rather upset to see me in such a state however. She spoke very little at first, making only idle chit-chat before moving onto more significant matters.

"So, I imagine you're wondering what happened. To be honest, we're not completely sure ourselves. I wonder, what was the last thing you remember?"

I couldn't respond, however my mind revisited

the incident. My memory was fuzzy; I could only recall the blast itself. Everything else had been buried deep within, never to surface. I'd been knocked unconscious and hadn't had the opportunity to witness the aftermath.

"I don't imagine you remember too much of what happened. It was all very sudden, after all."

She knotted her hands for a moment before continuing. "I enjoyed working with you and the rest of the crew in Kabul, Stephen. We made a great team. The rest of the team, or, at least, those that remain, are still in Kabul. I came back shortly after the incident however. As your personal assistant, it didn't make a whole lot of sense for me to stay if you weren't there."

For those that remain? What was that supposed to mean? I wanted her to elaborate, but was unable to ask. Instead, I listened intently.

"From what we've been able to gather, a bomb went off not too far from where you guys were shooting the story. William hadn't expected such a thing, and as a result, had been unable to plan for it. It went off suddenly and we lost all communication with you guys. The folks at the main station expressed great concern and tried for some time on the air to re-establish contact. The three of you have been in the news for the past few weeks now."

That was what I wanted to know. How had the others fared? Were Michael and Daniel all right? Had they made it out of there safely?

"We received a call from the producers at RBC headquarters shortly after we lost contact. They weren't certain, but believed that a nearby explosion had wrecked your gear. We were instructed to wait until the battle ceased before going to look for you guys. You know William, though. He planned a route and the rest of us set out immediately. It took us a little while to get there, however when we arrived, it was a terrible scene.

"Bombs were still going off and the gunfire still rang out. We searched and searched, trying our best to remain out of sight, but could find no trace of you. Finally however, we managed to find Michael and Daniel. I'm afraid they didn't make it, Stephen."

My blood froze. They hadn't made it?

"We found their bodies, but they didn't have pulses. Their bodies had been wreaked by the explosion, and they'd been scattered a great distance out from the site of the shoot. It was a miracle we found them at all."

I couldn't believe it. My crew members-- my friends, had been done in by that random act of violence. The two of them had been in Kabul before, and had felt confident in their abilities. That they'd been killed on duty seemed to me quite unbelievable. It made no sense. Why had I survived instead of them? I felt a profound guilt come over me as Ruth continued.

"We searched and searched for you, but to no avail, Stephen. Shortly thereafter we contacted the American embassy in Kabul and asked for their assistance. Paramedics were sent to the scene and they carried off Michael and Daniel. Thankfully, they arranged to have their bodies sent back to the U.S. and their families have since held funerals for them both. It's been rather somber about RBC in recent weeks as a result of all of this."

I couldn't get over the fact that Michael and Daniel had died. They'd been committed journalists who'd worked several times in Afghanistan. Their experience hadn't been enough to shield them from the monstrosities of war however. It pained me to see such experienced individuals needlessly killed. They'd been talented, reliable men, whose experience made them a comfort to novices such as myself in the field. More than that, they'd been good friends. They'd been welcoming to me and they'd helped me find my footing in a new position that would have otherwise been overwhelming. I couldn't stand it. Bad things have a way of happening to good people. To simply call the two of them good men would not have been enough however. They were dedicated journalists who'd died in the line of duty. They'd died while trying to bring the news to expectant, worried Americans. Their sacrifice had been enormous and I found myself filled with grief at their loss.

"As you can imagine, their funerals were gloomy. They both had families and this whole thing was totally unexpected. It wasn't their first time working in Kabul, after all. Nonetheless, the rest of the team hasn't been the same without them. They've all taken it very hard, and I suspect that they may come back to the States early as a result."

Ruth stood up and paced about the room a bit. "It took us a long time to find you, Stephen. We weren't sure what happened. The other two were some distance from where the shoot had been taking place, and we searched for you in that area. The violence continued to intensify however, and we were forced to return to the hotel. We made sure to search for you each day however. We couldn't bear the thought of you being injured and left for dead. Or, if you had died, we wanted at least for you to get a proper burial. For the most part, our news activities were put on hold and we joined in the search with volunteers from the embassy to find you. We spent two days in the hot sun searching for you. In the end however, our search was fruitless.

"It was by mere chance that an American soldier came upon you. You were found a short distance from the blast, and your body had been obscured somewhat by rubble. The soldier called for backup and had your body brought to the Army base in Kabul near the hotel.

They worked on identifying you for some time, before someone realized you were our missing journalist. There was a soldier at the base, Brian, I believe, who recognized you. They called the embassy and things moved forward from there.

"The soldiers were instructed by the people at the embassy to take you to a local hospital, however the place was small and unable to give you the care that you needed. Furthermore, the hospital itself had been damaged by a previous bombing and both staff and supplies were running dangerously low. It was quite a crisis. RBC headquarters wanted you brought here, to the Cleveland Clinic, but were unsure as to how to get you there. The staff at the small hospital worked on you and tried to make you stable. All of us came to visit you as well, and I have to say we were quite frightened. No one was sure whether you'd make it. RBC managed to arrange a flight back to the States with a group of soldiers who were returning. An army surgeon rode along with you, monitoring your vitals the whole way. You arrived and were promptly transported here, where you've been ever since. This is the ICU, Stephen."

Things were beginning to make sense. Although there yet existed blank spots in my memory, I had a better idea now of what had transpired after the blast. Still, I had questions.

"The doctor filled me in on your care as well. They immediately began sealing up your wounds when you arrived and they did a number of X-rays and CT's. They said you'd experienced a bit of brain swelling, but hadn't suffered any brain damage. A few bones had been broken, and your limbs had been severed. Aside from that however, the doctors seem to think that you'll make a full recovery. You're unable to speak due to both the stress of the incident and the blow to the head you suffered, however a bit of work with a speech therapist should help you with that. And although you're paralyzed at the moment, medical technology has come a long way. There are some great prosthetics you may be able to use. I know it's difficult, Stephen, but please don't lose hope. We're all in this together, and everyone at RBC, the rest of the crew and I included, are hoping to see you recover in the days to come. Whatever you do, please don't lose hope."

She wiped a trail of tears from her cheek and placed her hand on my shoulder. "Things will be alright, Stephen. I can't pretend to know what you're going through right now, but I promise you things will get better. You're in good hands here, and the doctors are moving forward, exploring treatments that will help you. You're alive, Stephen, and so long as you're alive, there's always hope."

I realized she was right. Although I'd been dealt a terrible hand, I was still alive. Rising above these injuries would take a lot of work; it would likely take every bit of focus I could muster. And yet, I no longer felt despair. The struggle no longer seemed insurmountable to me. I'd work as hard as possible, just as I had over the years to become a journalist, to re-gain some sense of normalcy in my life. Ruth was right. I was alive, which meant that I still had hope. Countless people were there to help me through the difficulties in my recovery; skilled doctors, dedicated friends, family and co-workers. How could I fail?

Ruth excused herself, but said she'd come back to visit tomorrow. "I'm afraid it's getting a bit late. I've got to get going, but I'm glad I had a chance to see you, Stephen. I'll let everyone know how you're doing. Get some rest and I'll see you tomorrow, alright?" She pulled on her jacket and began slowly for the door, pausing for a moment as she walked out to look back at me once more. She forced a smile. "Everything's going to be all right, Stephen. We'll help you along the way."

8

My recovery began very slowly. During my first days, I was visited by a speech pathologist who helped me regain my speech. He explained to me that the mental trauma, coupled with my injuries, had temporarily hampered my speech capabilities, however after a lengthy diagnostic process he declared that my speech would soon return. Sure enough, it did. Within a day of saying my first words, I was able to carry on a conversation just as I'd been able to do before the incident. The expert couldn't help but marvel at my recovery; it was not uncommon for patients of his to ease back into speech over a course of many days or even weeks. My recovery was among the swiftest he'd ever seen. The ability to speak eased a great deal of my suffering and made it easier for me to maintain a higher level of morale.

At the start, I was forced to remain in bed, speaking only with the rehabilitation professionals and urged to rest. The human body requires a tremendous amount of rest after weathering trauma, and as a result, I spent my days sleeping and visiting with various guests. My physician, Dr. Robert Crane, was a patient man. His daily visits continued, and he went about his routine with relative fluidity. During such visits, the two of us would converse for some time, and during my stay at the Cleveland Clinic, we became good friends.

"Things are looking good, Stephen," said Dr. Crane to me one afternoon as he finished his assessment. "Your vital signs have stabilized, and the nurses tell me your spirits have improved somewhat as well. At this rate, we'll be able to begin your rehabilitation quite soon. Perhaps next week. How does that sound?"

I smiled at him. "That sounds great, doc. I look forward to it. I've been stuck in this bed so long I've begun to forget what the outside world is like."

"I can only imagine," he replied. "You've been a good patient though, Stephen. Just do your best to stay positive and to rest during these last days before rehab begins. So long as your vitals remain stable, we'll look into getting you out of bed. Hang in there, and let the nurses know if you need anything at all."

"I will, doctor. Thanks." The staff at the hospital

had all been very friendly and accommodating to me. The nurses on each shift had proven very dedicated, and were always willing to assist me, no matter the hour. They'd been prompt in administering medications and changing dressings. The physicians had also been a friendly bunch. There were numerous consulting physicians working on my case, and although I could not remember all of their names, I'd been impressed with their professionalism and expertise.

As the doctor left the room, the day-shift nurse came in and gave me my daily course of antibiotics. "How are you feeling today?" she asked me.

"I'm feeling alright," I said. "Not a hundred percent just yet, but I'm getting there. Thanks for asking."

"Can I get you anything?" she asked, exchanging the bags on the IV pole.

"Well, if you don't mind, I wouldn't mind watching a little TV," I said.

"No problem." She walked across the room and

switched on the television. "Anything in particular you'd like to watch?"

I thought about it a minute. "How about the news? RBC, if possible."

She searched through the channels until she came upon the RBC station. "There you go. If you need anything else, let us know. We'll be in again shortly to check on you, Mr. Cook."

"Thanks!" I replied.

I watched the news for some time, drifting off during a weather broadcast. It seemed that the weather was set to improve during the week to come, with unseasonably high temperatures in the lower seventies. I hoped as I dozed off that I'd be able to spend some time outside during my rehab. It felt like such a long time since I'd been in the warm sunlight.

When I awoke, the news was still on. The 5 o'clock news had begun, and I noticed a familiar face on screen.

It was Ben Roberts; one of my favorite RBC

anchors. I recalled how I'd met him during my tour of RBC headquarters in New York City, and I watched him go through the day's headlines. There was talk of the stock market, the war in Afghanistan and other items of international interest. Surprisingly however, another story was featured among the headlines. Something I wasn't expecting.

"RBC correspondent Stephen Cook is recuperating in Cleveland, Ohio," he said. "As many of you viewers are aware, he was among the victims of a blast while reporting on-site in Kabul, Afghanistan. Sources tell us he is still resting; however his recovery seems to be underway. We'll fill you in on the details as they become available. This is an important story for us here at RBC, and I hope that you'll join us in keeping Stephen Cook in your thoughts and prayers."

I was flattered. It was surreal listening to Ben Roberts talk about me on the evening news. Around the time the broadcast ended, the nurse came in to change my dressings.

The dressing changes were time-consuming.

The old bandages were removed slowly, one at a time, and the wounds had to be cleansed. The first few times, it had been hard to watch. The removal of the bandages acquainted me with a sight I would have to get used to; the stubs from which my limbs had once extended. The nurse was careful in her work however, and cleansed the wounds quickly and efficiently. When the wounds were clean, she would set to re-wrapping each of them in fresh bandages.

"Your wounds are looking good, Mr. Cook. There appears to be no sign of infection. You're lucky; I've seen patients have limbs removed only to develop gangrene. You seem to be healing up very nicely however. When the wounds are fully healed, you'll be able to start rehab with the physical therapists."

"I'm looking forward to it," I told her.

The nurse informed me as she finished the dressing change that I had a guest. "I believe she said her name was Ruth? She's been here to visit you before."

"Oh, yes. Please send her in."

The nurse left the room and Ruth was allowed to enter.

"Hello, Stephen," she said, taking a seat at my bedside. "How are things today?"

"Better," I replied. "I've still got a long way to go, but with each day that passes, I feel better and better."

She smiled. "Well, that's what's important. Baby steps, you know? You've been through a lot, so take your time to recover."

"So," I began, "I was just watching the 5 o'clock news. You aren't going to believe this-- Ben Roberts did a story on me! He informed the viewers that I was recovering and touched briefly upon the incident. It was really something else! I never thought I'd ever hear him do a story on me."

"You should have seen the news after the incident," she said. "For a while, the other headlines took a backseat to your story, Stephen. The staff at RBC have taken this whole thing very seriously, and believe it or not, the viewers are invested in you as well."

"Well, I suppose you're right," I said. "Still, it was a surprise to watch a story about myself on the news. I've seen videos of myself anchoring in the past and I've been approached by people who recognize me from TV, but watching someone talk about me on the national news is something completely different. It kind of makes me feel like a celebrity," I chuckled.

"I know what you mean," she replied. "Anyway Stephen, I came here with some exciting news!"

"Oh? What is it?"

"Well, the folks at RBC have arranged for your parents to come to Cleveland. They'll be staying at a nearby hotel so that they can come and visit you!"

"That's great!" I said. And yet, as I pondered her words, an uneasiness came over me.

"What's the matter, Stephen?" Ruth asked, noticing the change in my expression.

"Well, it's just that I don't really know how to feel about seeing my parents. I mean, sure, I'll be happy to see them and I'm sure that they're worried to death about me. But at the same time, I'd promised them that I'd stay safe while in Afghanistan. To have them see me like this is, well, not at all ideal. I feel guilty, Ruth. My mother is going to take it especially hard, I expect."

"Oh, Stephen," said Ruth. "Your parents will be very happy to see you, and I'm sure that they're just happy that you're alive. Don't feel guilty. What happened was totally unexpected. It isn't as though you went and did this on purpose, after all. Your parents will certainly be sad to hear about your injuries, but in the end I think it will do you good to see them."

"I suppose you're right," I agreed. "When are they arriving?"

"If I'm not mistaken, they should be arriving sometime tomorrow. Mr. Sawyer himself arranged the trip and is handling their airfare and lodging. He called them up and offered to fly them out. I've never seen him do anything like it. I think he may be coming out to visit at some point as well, however I think he wants to give you a chance to recover somewhat first."

"That's great to hear. Please be sure to pass on

my thanks to Mr. Sawyer. This is very generous of him."

"I will," she replied.

Ruth talked for a brief while about the weather. "You should see it out there. It's warm, and the sun is just about to set. The colors in the sky are really something else."

"I'd love to see it. Of course, I can't really get out of bed right now to take a look," I said with a laugh. "I look forward to spending some time outdoors in the days to come, though. Perhaps they'll be able to work a little outdoor time into my rehab."

"That'd be nice," she said. "You know, maybe there *is* a way for you to see the sunset."

"Oh? What do you have in mind?"

Ruth excused herself into the hallway and had a brief talk with the nurse. The two of them entered the room a short time later and maneuvered my bed into the hallway outside my room. "The view from this window is quite good," said Ruth as they stationed my bed in the hall. The nurse grappled with my IV pole and made sure that it was running properly.

I peered out of the large hallway window. The sun was slowly setting over the city and streaks of bright orange radiated about the trees and nearby buildings. It had been so long since I'd seen the outside world with my own eyes.

"What do you think?" asked Ruth.

"It's beautiful," I said. "It makes me look forward to finally getting out of here."

She nodded.

Watching the sun set over Cleveland made my heart pound with fervor. This would not be the last sunset I'd see; I'd work as hard as possible to recover so that I could soon enjoy the world's beauty once more. Feeling motivated, a thrill came over me.

"Goodness, what's going on over here?" asked the nurse as an alarm on my bed began to ring. "Your heart rate seems to have gone up considerably. Be careful not to get too excited, Mr. Cook!"

I laughed. "I'm sorry. It's really quite a sight, though. After all I've been through, something so simple as a sunset feels really special to me."

The nurse smiled and patted me on the chest. "We're going to work hard to ensure that you can see many more like it."

The sun finally set and the nurse wheeled my bed back into the room. Ruth left a short time later and I watched a movie on TV until sleep overcame me.

***

The next afternoon, my parents arrived in Cleveland. Hurriedly securing their lodging, they took a cab to the hospital and were escorted to my room. I saw my mother first, peering sheepishly inside after a light knock.

"Come on in, mom," I said.

She smiled weakly and ambled inside. My father followed close behind. From the doorway, the nurse offered them both a seat in the room and then closed the door for our privacy.

"Thanks for coming to visit," I told them. "I'm happy to see you guys."

My parents said nothing for some time. They smiled and I sensed some degree of relief in them, however they seemed at a loss for words. For a while they sought out something to say, but were unable to find anything appropriate for the situation. Instead, I led them into conversation.

"First time in Cleveland?"

The two of them laughed a quiet, polite laugh. This visit was difficult for them, no doubt.

"I'm glad you're alive, Stephen," said my dad, his gaze hanging low.

My mother nodded in agreement.

"We were actually watching the news when the bomb went off. I have to tell you, I've never had such a fright in my life. I think that my heart actually skipped a beat or two; I very nearly had your mother drive me to the emergency room," said my dad with a slight grin.

I bit my lip, overcome with guilt. I felt terrible that I'd caused them so much stress and worry. "I'm sorry," I blurted out, looking away for a moment. I couldn't bring myself to look either of them in the eye for fear that I might break down into a fit of tears.

My mother wicked at her eyes with a handkerchief. "No, Stephen. There's no need to apologize. If anything, we're sorry for not having arrived sooner."

"It's all right, mom. I'm just happy that you guys are here now."

My dad continued. "I'm glad they brought you here. This is one of the best hospitals in the country. When I heard that you'd been transferred to the Cleveland Clinic, I felt confident that they'd be able to take good care of you. How have things been?"

"The food could be better," I laughed.

I noticed my mother looking me over subtly from her spot across from the bed. I spied a terrible uneasiness in her gaze. She'd probably heard about the extent of my injuries, but seeing them in person had prompted an altogether more serious response. Seeing her son in such a state was probably very difficult for her.

"Does it hurt?" my mother managed to ask.

I shook my head. "It did for a while, but things have improved, mom. It's like dad said, they're taking good care of me here. The pain medications have been given on time and I've been resting. When I first awoke I was in excruciating pain. In fact, I wasn't even able to speak. I've come a long way since then, though. Soon enough, I'll be in rehab. When rehab's complete, I'll see what options are available to me."

My dad smiled with pride. "Even after all you've been through, your spirit's still intact. I knew I hadn't raised a quitter. I don't think anyone could fault you, after the things you've weathered, for giving up on life. And yet, here you are, planning your rehabilitation. It's inspiring, Stephen." Up to that point, I'd never seen my father cry. His tears filled me with a certain unease. For my whole life, he'd always been a tough, authoritative figure. Certainly he'd been a good father, however he'd never been overly emotional. As he wiped away his tears, I felt myself overcome with sadness however.

"I've worked too hard to just roll over and die," I said, forcing a smile. It gave way to a brief series of sobs however, and we sat in silence for a long while as I sought to compose myself.

My dad patted me on the head. "Mr. Sawyer at RBC has been very supportive during this time. He's arranged for us to stay at a nearby hotel for as long as we like, and we intend to stay as long as you need us here, Stephen. If you're dedicated to recovery, we want to be here for you. If there's anything you need, we'll be there right behind you. Alright?"

"Thanks, dad."

My mother, pale with worry, agreed. "This whole thing has had me so worried; I hadn't put much thought into your recovery. It's like your father says, though. We'll be there for you. No matter what you need, we'll be there with you every step of the way."

"Have you guys spoken to uncle Jim?" I asked. "Be sure to let him know I'm alright."

"We will," my dad replied. "I was planning to give him a call tonight to fill him in."

My parents stayed a short while longer before retiring to their hotel for the night. "Sleep well, Stephen. We've left our phone number with the nurse, in case you need anything. Feel free to call, no matter the time. We'll be back to visit tomorrow," said my father.

"All right," I said. "Have a good night, guys."

As they left, I sighed with relief. It had been good to see them and to know that I had their support. I slept somewhat comfortably that night, my mind filled with memories of childhood and family.

***

The next afternoon, my parents returned to visit with a special guest. Even before they came to the door, I could hear a familiar clatter ringing through the hall. My mother nudged the door to my room open and Max scurried in, barking repeatedly at me from the side of the bed.

"Max!" I exclaimed.

"We thought you might want to spend a little time with ol' Max," said my mother, pulling back on his leash somewhat. "We asked Dr. Crane if it'd be alright to bring the dog inside. Ordinarily they only make exceptions for service animals. The doctor thought it might do you some good to see the dog however, so he OK'd it. It looks like Max has missed you! He just made the flight from Kabul. We picked him up at the airport this morning."

My mother placed the dog up on the bed, where he curled up at my side. It pleased me to see him safe and sound; in the days after the accident in Kabul, I'd completely forgotten about him. My dad shuffled in and scratched the dog's belly.

"You should have seen the nurses," he said with a chuckle. "They acted like they'd never seen a dog before. Each of them had to stop to pet him. Of course, old Max here handled it like a champ."

I grinned. "Things have been so hectic recently, I'd very nearly forgotten about him. Who made the arrangements for him to return to the States?"

"It was your crew in Kabul. It seems that they're returning home, and in the process they arranged for Max to come along. I'm sure several of your crew members will probably show up for a visit in the weeks to come," said my dad.

"That sounds great!" I said. "I hope they're all doing well."

My parents returned to their hotel for a brief while but left Max behind. The poor dog, probably jet-lagged somewhat from the lengthy flight, joined me for my afternoon nap that day.

***

Some days later, I was paid a visit by members of the crew. William was the first. He arrived in the early evening one day in rather poor spirits.

"Hello, Stephen," he said as he arrived. I invited him to take a seat, however he refused and chose to stand instead. "I won't take up too much of your time," he continued. "I know you're unwell and you need your rest. I just came to apologize."

"What for?" I asked.

He laughed. "What for? Well, isn't it obvious? If I'd done a better job, none of this would have happened. If I'd only been a better security advisor, perhaps we wouldn't have lost two men and you wouldn't be in this state. I had to return to the States; I just couldn't bring myself to work out there anymore. After all I've done, I don't trust myself to keep others safe any longer."

"William, that's unfair," I replied. "I don't blame you for anything. What happened back in Kabul, well, it was a fluke. None of us could have known."

"Maybe so, but I still feel as though I should have done more. Maybe chosen another location. Something."

I sighed. "What happened was very unfortunate. We lost some good friends that day, William. But I know they wouldn't want you to beat yourself up over things like this. The whole crew trusted you with their lives, William, and you did your best to keep us out of harm's way. You did everything you could to protect us, so don't feel guilty. If anything, it was my fault for insisting on getting a better look at the fight below the ridge."

He peered out the window with intensity. "I don't know, Stephen. The others who were caught in the blast-- they had families. What about them? Somehow, I'm still coming to terms with what happened. Why is it that those good men had to die in the line of duty? And why couldn't I see it coming? Why couldn't I prevent it?"

"Well," I replied, "I'm afraid I don't know the answer to those questions. But in the past weeks, I've learned a little something about healing, William. I've been confined to this bed and I've had a lot of time to think about what's happened. Take time to sort out your feelings on the matter, but do your best to allay that guilt of yours. It's unhealthy."

He nodded. "Perhaps it is."

"At any rate, it's going to take a long time for all of this to sink in. I'm still trying to come to terms with things myself. Healing is a process; it doesn't happen overnight. Take some time off and reflect upon what's happened, but whatever you do, I want you to promise me one thing."

"Oh? What's that?" he asked.

"I want you to return to your job as a security advisor. It's what you're good at, William, and you'd be doing many good journalists a disservice by quitting it altogether."

William smiled. "I appreciate that." He paced about the room briefly before continuing. "I plan to take some time off, but perhaps I'll return in the autumn. In the meantime, I want to make myself available to you, Stephen. Your healing isn't just mental like mine, but it's physical as well. I want to help you in any way I can. Please let me know if there's anything I can do."

"Sure thing, William. Thanks."

He said goodbye and left in somewhat higher spirits than when he'd arrived.

Glenda and Ruth visited the next day, and

brought me a lovely get-well card. Their visit was brief, but I appreciated it nonetheless.

"I think I'll be taking a post here in the States. Somehow I don't feel like returning to Afghanistan. Perhaps someday I'll change my mind, but for right now I'm content to do work here in the U.S." said Glenda.

"I can't say I blame you. Do you have anything in mind?"

"Well, I've spoken to some of the folks at headquarters and they seem to believe that some new positions will be opening up soon. I may look into one of those. I want to stay with RBC, so I'll see what opportunities are available in the near future."

I reflected that day upon the demise of my trusted crew members. I had my mother write a brief letter of condolence to their families and asked her to deliver it. However slight, I felt it necessary to make some gesture to demonstrate my sadness at their passing. I regretted not being able to go to their funerals; however, considering the state of things, I was in no condition to attend.

With my rehabilitation on the horizon, I couldn't help but marvel at the multitude of people I had to support me. Everyone in my life had come together to help me during my time of need, and I felt all the stronger and more motivated for their support. Very soon, I would need to focus on the task of rehabilitation, and I knew I'd be surrounded all the while with people I could depend on for support. Ordinarily, I might've been afflicted with fear at the uncertainty of such a situation as mine. However, considering the support system I had, I no longer saw any reason to fear. More than anything, I was excited to be moving towards normalcy once more.

9

Dr. Crane came to visit me on a rainy Thursday. I was peering out the window at the falling rain when he knocked on my door and entered. "How are you feeling today?" he asked me.

"Fine," I said. "The pain is very nearly gone."

"That's good, that's good. I think that tomorrow we're going to begin your treatment. I've scheduled a meeting with a physical therapist for you. They'll determine your range of motion and see about fitting you with prosthetics, if you're interested. I'll be consulting with some other experts to see about other options for mobility. With any luck, you'll be out of the hospital within a week or so."

I was thrilled. "That's great news, doctor. Thanks."

"No problem. I'll be in to see you tomorrow after your meeting with the physical therapist. Let me know how it all goes," he said.

The remainder of the day was spent in relative

excitement. I told my parents the news; that I'd be starting rehab the next day, and that the doctor was looking at options for my mobility. "Things won't be quite the same, of course, but I'm going to do my best to make sure that I can maintain my quality of life."

My parents agreed. "So long as you're comfortable and mobile enough to live a life that's fulfilling to you, we'll be happy," said my father.

The next morning, I met the physical therapist. He did a number of exercises with me to determine whether or not I had any mobility whatsoever.

"It would seem," he said after some study, "that you have virtually no range of motion. Your limbs were almost completely severed, and I'm afraid that what remains-- the trunks-- aren't sufficient for locomotion. Prosthetics will probably be more for cosmetic value than actual movement."

I had expected as much. "Alright, so what are my options for mobility?"

"Well, there are many options. There are some

automated wheelchairs you might be interested in. They're highly maneuverable, even for someone such as yourself. The controls are intuitive and I'm sure you could have it figured out in no time. Does something like that interest you?"

I nodded. "That sounds interesting, yes. I'd like to try one out, if possible."

"All right, then. I'll have to discuss the options with Dr. Crane, however I expect he'll have no problem with such a thing. I'll also see about getting you fitted with high-quality prosthetics. Sound good?"

I smiled. "It sure does. I can't wait to get out of here."

The therapist left and talked with the doctor, who entered my room a short while later. "Automated wheelchair? That would do nicely, I think. Tomorrow we'll have you fitted for the prosthetics and we'll have the order placed immediately. Ordinarily it would take a few weeks for the prosthetics to be shipped to us, however I'll make certain to put a rush on this order. You've been with us a long while, Stephen. I hate to see you go, but

I'm sure you'll be very happy to leave."

I laughed. "I certainly will be happy to go home. Not that I won't miss some aspects of this place, though. You and the nurses have been great. I really appreciate everything you've done for me."

"It's no problem at all, Stephen. I just wish all of my other patients were as pleasant as you are."

We chatted for a while longer before he continued on his rounds through the hospital.

***

A representative from the prosthetic company arrived to take measurements of my body. "We've got to make sure we get a good fit; not too tight, not too loose."

He measured the circumference of my stubs and marked down the values in a notepad. He took each measurement twice, to make certain that he'd been accurate. When it was through, he marked on my skin in black marker the areas where the prosthetics would fit. He explained to me the materials used in their production and the sort of lining that they would feature to ensure my comfort.

"I see that the doctor has put in a rush order for these pieces, so I'm going to deliver the measurements right away and have the people at the company get started on them. You can expect to see me here again in a day or two. I'll be helping you put them on, and I'll also teach you how to maintain them at that point."

Later in the day, the physical therapist paid me another visit to discuss options for bodily support. "Because you'll no longer have full legs to support you while in a seated position, I would recommend using a custom back-support in tandem with the wheelchair. There are numerous shapes and options, and if you're interested, I can have one ordered alongside the wheelchair."

"That sounds great," I replied.

"All right, I'll order an ergonomic model and we'll see how you like it."

Things were moving forward. Some weeks ago, I'd despaired, wondering whether my life had come to an end. Now, I was making strides towards the future. The wheelchair and prosthetics would be arriving within the next few days, and when I'd mastered their use, I'd be free to leave the hospital.

The physical therapist taught me some basic stretches I could do to strengthen and relieve my back muscles. "You'll be relying on your back more often now. You still have some movement there, so it's important to work those muscles just a bit." He was a helpful person, and remained patient as I sought to reacquaint myself with movement.

When he was through, he asked me if I wanted to visit the outside. I agreed enthusiastically and he had one of the nurses help him strap me into a specialized wheelchair. We began through the halls and down the elevator to the lobby. Leaving the lobby, I felt a gust of warm wind sweep against my body. Somehow, it made me feel free. It seemed as though the air I'd been breathing-- the air I'd been immersed in for several weeks-- had been unclean or synthetic by comparison.

"It's a nice day out, don't you agree?" he said to

me as we left the building.

I nodded and reveled in the warmth of the sun. "It's been so long since I've been outside. The last time I remember being in the sun, I was in Kabul. The days out there are really, really hot. The sunlight wasn't at all pleasant there. It was something you had to try and escape from to stay comfortable."

"That sounds rough."

We stayed outside for a long while. Naturally, I wasn't terribly enthusiastic about returning to my room, however I had little choice in the matter. The therapist wheeled me back upstairs and I was settled back into my bed. I thanked him as he left and took a brief nap.

***

When the prosthetics arrived, I was pleased to find them rather life-like. They'd been forged of a rubbery material that resembled human skin both in appearance and texture. Each piece, which had been built to my body's exact specifications, was fitted closely to my stubs with straps and clamps. They proved surprisingly comfortable and convincing.

"The technology's come a long way," the representative said as he helped me strap on the prosthetics. "I help to build the things and even I have to do a double take from time to time. They're quite lifelike. And they're sturdy as well. So long as you take good care of them, you won't need to buy another set for the rest of your life."

He explained how to maintain the prosthetics and how to ensure that they were worn correctly. He also explained the process to my parents, who arrived during his visit. "It's better that you all know how to work these things," he said.

Later that day, the wheelchair was delivered. The physical therapist arrived and taught me how to use it. As he'd said, the system proved quite simple and provided me with a decent range of movement. Furthermore, it was battery-powered and required only a daily charge of a few hours.

I experimented with the wheelchair controls until I felt that I could adequately control it. Turning about in my room, I felt, for the first time in weeks, like a normal person. I was mobile once again, and the prosthetics were convincing.

"I can't believe how far technology has come," said my dad as he marveled at the wheelchair. "That thing looks like it'll turn on a dime. And those prosthetics-- if I didn't know any better, I'd say those were your real feet poking out of your pant-leg. It's really something else."

It was late in the day by the time I'd grown comfortable with my new gear. The nurses would need time to prepare my discharge paperwork, and so I opted to stay a final night at the hospital. My parents would arrive in the morning to pick me up.

Dr. Crane came in that evening to say goodbye. "As of right now, you're ready to go home. We just have to finalize all of the bureaucratic stuff on our end and you'll be on your way in the morning. When you were first brought in, I wasn't sure that you were going to make it. Looking back on it now, though, I can see that there was never any doubt. You're a hard worker,

Stephen, and you've got a lot of character. Your will to live is very strong, and I wish you luck in your future endeavors."

I thanked the doctor heartily. "Thank you for all you've done, doctor. I wouldn't have made it without you. The entire staff has been so helpful to me over the past weeks. I can't really convey to you just how grateful I am."

"There's no need," he replied with a smile. "We're all just happy to see you well once again."

The doctor signed off on my discharge orders and said goodbye. Various other staff members shuffled in throughout the course of the evening to say their goodbyes as well. I'd come to know so many of them over my stay; each of them had contributed directly to my care and had become friends. I thanked them each for all they'd done.

***

I slept well during my last night in the hospital. In the morning, the nurse came in and went over my discharge instructions. When I'd received everything she had to give me I made my way down to the lobby to wait for my parents. They pulled up in their van and helped me inside.

We drove to their hotel and relaxed there for some time, uncertain of where to go next. As we lounged about, my mother received a call.

"Hello? Oh, Mr. Sawyer, how are you?"

It was Mr. Sawyer, RBC's president. What was he calling about? Perhaps to inquire after my condition?

The call ended quickly. "Mr. Sawyer would like to come visit you, Stephen. He'll be in Cleveland later today, he said. Do you feel well enough for guests?"

"Absolutely," I replied. "Where would he like to meet?"

"He said he'll meet us here and that he'll call when he's close."

"All right, that sounds fine," I said.

Some hours later, we received another call from

Mr. Sawyer, this time telling us that he was near the hotel. We met him in the main lobby and took a seat in a small, private lounge. "Stephen," he said to me as he walked in, "it's been a while. How are you feeling?"

"Not too bad, Mr. Sawyer. Thanks for asking."

"You've made a great recovery, I see. The viewers will be happy to hear that you're feeling well, I'm sure. I'll let the folks back at the station know that you've been released and are doing well. In fact, if you'd be willing, I'd love to have you on the news one of these days. The viewers would probably love to hear about your experiences and recovery."

"I'd like that," I replied.

"Oh, that reminds me." Mr. Sawyer pulled a card from his briefcase. "This arrived a few days ago. It's from your old crew in Detroit." He opened the card and read to me the comments that everyone had written.

"Be sure to tell them I said thanks. Perhaps I'll stop by the old station for a visit one of these days."

"Certainly," said Mr. Sawyer.

My parents decided to go for a walk so that Mr. Sawyer and I could talk in private. When we were alone, Mr. Sawyer continued. "I'm sorry I didn't come to visit you sooner. I simply wanted to make sure that you'd recovered. The last thing a recovering patient needs is a meddling boss visiting."

"Not at all," I said. "I wouldn't have minded, I assure you."

He smiled. "Well, at any rate, I've come to discuss a few things with you, Stephen. Namely, what are your plans now? It seems that you're doing well and have made up for the mobility you lost in the blast. Nonetheless, you'll no longer be able to fill the post of foreign correspondent. What are your plans for the future?"

I paused a moment. "Well, things are still falling into place. I'm trying to take it one day at a time, so I'm not altogether sure what's to come. I'd like to continue my career in journalism, but I admit that my current state makes for some difficulties."

"That's true," he said with a nod. "If there's

anything I can do to accommodate you, please let me know. I'll do whatever I must to keep you at RBC. You're a dedicated journalist and we certainly don't want to lose you."

"Thanks," I said. "I'll be sure to let you know as soon as I decide."

"Well, as I mentioned earlier, I'd like to feature you on the news. Let me know when you're available and I'll arrange it."

"That'd be great," I said. "I'll let you know in the next few days."

Mr. Sawyer sat silently for a moment. "You know," he began, "it's a miracle you made it, Stephen. Your recovery is a testament to both the wonders of modern medicine and your strong desire to survive. I knew I'd hired the right man when I sent you to Kabul. Of course, I wish you'd never been injured. In some ways I feel responsible for what happened to you and the other members of your crew, since it was me who sent you all in the first place."

"Mr. Sawyer, it was a dangerous job, but someone had to do it. I feel honored to have done so. If such a thing had to happen to me, I'm just happy it was in the line of duty, while I was doing something important to me. Someone has to bring news about the war to the American people, and had I not been knocked out of commission, I'd still be in Kabul doing just that."

He smiled. "You know, I expected you to say something along those lines. You're a thoughtful man, Stephen. In the near future, I hope to have you working for us in New York again. I can't make any promises yet, but some positions will be opening up in the near future. If you're interested in furthering your career, I'll always have a place for you, Stephen."

"I'm glad to hear that. Working with you guys at RBC has been a dream come true for me. Although things have been difficult for me recently, I'm looking on the bright side. I'm alive, my mind is intact, and, save for some minor troubles, I'm still mobile. Overall, I feel very fortunate."

"Indeed," he said. "I suppose it could have turned

out much worse."

Mr. Sawyer and I chatted until dark, when he excused himself for the night. "Call me if you want to be on the news, Stephen. There are a lot of people out there eager to hear from you."

10

I arranged with Mr. Sawyer to appear on the evening news. I would be interviewed by Ben Roberts about my experiences in Kabul and about my lengthy recovery. My parents and I were flown in from Cleveland to RBC headquarters in New York City. Mr. Sawyer was waiting for us when we arrived.

"It's good to see you all," he told us as we entered the lobby. "Are you ready, Stephen?"

"I am," I replied. We made our way to studio A, which was bustling with pre-broadcast excitement. As I entered, several of the staff members came up to me and asked me how I was doing. "I'm fine," I said again and again. One of the technicians clipped a microphone to my shirt and led me to the set.

"Go ahead and get situated there next to the anchor's desk. We'll be doing your segment first, ahead of the day's headlines."

I was somewhat surprised that my story had taken precedence. I made my way to the desk and had a brief chat with Ben Roberts prior to the broadcast. He was every bit as cordial as he had been during our first meeting, and expressed interest in interviewing me about my experiences.

The crew prepared for the broadcast and, when everything was set, began at once.

"Good evening, I'm Ben Roberts with RBC news. We've got some big news for our viewers today; we've got RBC journalist Stephen Cook here in studio with us. For those of you who don't recall Mr. Cook, he was our foreign correspondent in Kabul, Afghanistan. He was heavily injured by a blast in the mountains that claimed the lives of two of his crew members. He's here today to fill us in on the details of his work in Afghanistan, as well as to describe to us his recovery."

The producer motioned to me from the side-lines. It was my turn to introduce myself. "Hello, I'm Stephen Cook, former RBC foreign affairs correspondent in Kabul, Afghanistan. It's a pleasure to be here."

Ben began his interview forthwith. "It's good to have you, Stephen. Many of us have been concerned for you over the past several weeks, and we're all glad to see that you've recovered. Please, give us your impressions about Afghanistan."

I took a moment to think about it. "Well Ben, Afghanistan is a fine country. I spent only a brief while there, but all things considered, I enjoyed it. There is a lot of tension in the region, and I feel that my crew and I managed to capture that to some degree through our reporting. Nonetheless, the people there carry on as they do anywhere else. They don't let the fighting get in the way of their happiness, and I met many inspiring individuals in Kabul who worked very hard in the face of senseless violence. It was a very eye-opening experience."

Ben nodded. "I see, and can you explain to us what it was like that day in the mountains? What went through your mind after the blast? Did you have any warning prior to the detonation?"

"Admittedly, I can't remember the incident too well," I laughed. "It's difficult to remember."

"Why's that?" he asked.

"Well, it's kind of like getting hit by a bomb."

Ben laughed heartily. "I imagine the experience was quite traumatic, then. It makes sense that your understanding of the events would be limited."

"Yes, the blast was tremendous, and I remember very little overall. I do remember hearing a member of my crew in my earpiece. I also recall the blinding white light that overcame me as the bomb went off. Aside from those details and some other varied memory fragments, I remember nothing."

"So, the blast was quite a surprise, then? There was no forewarning?"

"None at all. We thought the area was safe, but it seems we miscalculated. You can't always predict things like that in war. Sure enough, we were just unlucky."

"I see. And so, as I understand it, you were injured in the blast rather heavily. What was the extent of your injuries, Stephen?"

"For starters, I lost my limbs. That's the most significant injury I weathered."

Ben's eyes grew wide. "What? But, I'm looking at your arms and legs right now."

"No, they're prosthetics," I replied. They're custom-made, so I understand the confusion."

"So, you lost your limbs. Goodness, that must have been terrible, Stephen. I can't imagine what that must have been like. What other injuries did you sustain?"

"I took a blow to the head and had a bit of brain swelling. A few of my vital organs were also bruised. Some bones were broken as well. All in all, I was in really, really bad shape. Or so I've been told by the physicians who took care of me."

"That's right; initial reports made it sound as though you'd been mortally wounded and wouldn't survive. We received word that you'd been treated at a local hospital in Kabul, but that you were to be transferred to the Cleveland Clinic here in the States. Tell me, how was your care?"

"My care was fantastic," I said. "The doctors and

nurses all worked together to keep me comfortable. They were understanding throughout the whole process and they kept me informed of my status and my options for treatment. Overall, I was very satisfied with my care."

"That's good to hear," he said. "And so, moving forward, what can we expect from Stephen Cook in the future?" Will you be joining us here at RBC again? Do you have something else lined up, or are you planning to go into early retirement?"

"Well," I said, looking for the right words, "right now, everything's on the table. I'm not too sure about what I want to do. I've considered returning to RBC in some capacity, however I don't know what duties I'd be able to fill. I've also considered retiring, however I'm still young-- I've worked hard to get here and reporting the news has always been pleasurable work to me. I wouldn't want to stop."

"And we wouldn't want you to, either. You're an important member of the RBC family and the crew, as well as our viewers, have come to rely on you for quality news. I'm sure I'm not alone in hoping that you'll stay with us. Whatever you choose though, we wish you the best of luck, Stephen. We'll be cheering you on and keeping an eye out for you in the future."

"Thanks, Ben. I appreciate your interest and I'd like to thank all of our wonderful viewers for their concern. The outpouring of support has been huge, and it's helped me through some very difficult times. I couldn't have done it without them."

When the interview was over, I made my way off of the set and to the sidelines where I watched the rest of the broadcast.

"You did great," said Mr. Sawyer. "I could certainly see you up there anchoring, Stephen."

I laughed. "That'd be wonderful, Mr. Sawyer. I told you; I've always wanted to be an anchor at the main station. It'd be a dream come true."

During the broadcast, viewers had begun to flood RBC's social media websites with messages for me. Many of the messages were notes of support, asking me to continue on with RBC news. One comment particularly touched me. "RBC won't be the same without you, Stephen Cook. Please come back and help make the news interesting. You've got a rare talent for journalism, and no disability can put a damper on it."

I appreciated the tremendous support of the viewers. Their messages were validation for me; proof that all of the work I'd done over the years had made me a skilled journalist. It would be a shame, I realized, for me not to utilize those skills.

After the broadcast, I mingled with the crew a while and followed Mr. Sawyer to his office. "So, Stephen, did you enjoy your interview?"

"I did, thank you. I appreciate the opportunity."

Mr. Sawyer smiled. "You know, I hear a rumor that one of our anchors is looking to retire. I don't want to say anything too early, however if that position were to become available in the next few months, would you consider filling it, Stephen?"

My heart skipped a beat. "Well, I'm not sure, Mr. Sawyer. I mean, it's a lot of responsibility. I'm not sure whether I'm capable of filling such a role anymore. It would certainly be difficult."

"It would be difficult, yes. But not impossible. The crew here would work very hard to accommodate you, and as you can see, our viewers love you. I think you'd make a great fit for the position."

I thought it over a while. "Well, like I told you before, it's something of a dream job for me. If you were to offer me such a position, I'd consider it very seriously."

"I'm glad to hear that. I'll be sure to keep an ear out. If such a job should become available, you'll be my first pick for it."

I left RBC headquarters that evening feeling rather excited. I'd been interviewed by one of my all-time favorite anchors and had been informed of the possibility of a new position. There were so many things buzzing about my mind that I very nearly rolled by my parents without noticing them. We made our way to a hotel and rented a large suite, where the three of us spent the next few days relaxing. I wanted to be near RBC headquarters, in case Mr. Sawyer needed to speak with me about anything.

I spoke with my uncle Jim over the phone during our stay, and informed him of the possibility of a new position. He expressed excitement and relayed how thankful he was that I'd survived the incident in Afghanistan. Max had been sent to live with him until I could come up with a permanent living situation of my own. I could hear him barking in the background as we spoke on the phone.

"Tell Max I said hello," I told my uncle as he attempted to quiet the dog.

"Oh, I will," he laughed. "Max and I can't wait to see you again, Stephen."

"I'll be visiting you guys soon enough," I said. "Just as soon as I've got everything straightened out."

"Well, I look forward to it. You're welcome any time."

"Thanks, uncle Jim. Have a good one."

My mother hung up the phone and helped me

get settled into bed. "It's been a long day, honey. How about you get some rest? After all, you've only been out of the hospital a short time. It would be bad to overwork you right now."

I assured her that I felt fine. "It's nothing I can't handle, mom. I spent so much time in the hospital resting that I can't seem to stay still now. I've got to go out and seize the day-- make up for lost time!"

"There'll be plenty of time for that, I promise you," she said.

We spent the night in the hotel, watching old movies. It was a refreshing change of pace for all three of us, who'd been caught up in travel over the past few days.

***

Mr. Sawyer contacted me one morning as my family and I were considering a return to Detroit. The call came early, as we were packing up our belongings in the hotel. My mother brought the phone over to me. "It's Mr. Sawyer," she said, placing the receiver to my ear.

"Hello, Mr. Sawyer?"

"Yes, hello, Stephen," he said. "How are you this morning? I'm sorry to have called so early. I wanted to get ahold of you before you left, however."

"It's no problem at all, Mr. Sawyer. What can I help you with?"

"I've got some exciting news for you, Stephen. I'd like to meet with you and your parents, if possible. Are you all free this afternoon? We can meet at the station over lunch. Afterward, we'll head to my office to talk."

"That'd be fine," I said, taking a moment to explain Mr. Sawyer's plan to my mother. "We'll be there around eleven o'clock." I was excited to hear that he had news for me and suspected that it had to do with a new position. "I wonder, Mr. Sawyer, if this has something to do with a new position for me at RBC headquarters?"

He chuckled. "It does, yes. I don't want to give away too many of the details just yet however. In good time! I'll see you at the station cafeteria, then?"

"Sure thing. See you then." I went over the day's

plans with my parents and they helped me change my clothes and bathe. When we were through, we loaded our bags in my father's rental car and began for the station. Things had taken a bit longer than anticipated; I still wasn't used to relying on others for help in everyday matters, and as a result, was poor at gauging the amount of time each task required. It was a bit past eleven when we finally arrived at the station. I rolled into the lobby, greeted the secretary and led my parents down the hall to the cafeteria.

I spied Mr. Sawyer sitting at a table in the corner of the sparsely populated cafeteria. Here and there staff members ambled about ordering their lunches. By the looks of it, the cafeteria had only just opened.

Mr. Sawyer stood and greeted us warmly. "Stephen, it's good to see you." He turned to my parents and shook their hands. "Please, take a seat, folks. What can I get you?" My parents ordered simple lunches and sat around the table, eating and making conversation.

"I can't believe the traffic in this city," said my father as we ate. "And here I thought downtown Detroit was bad!"

Mr. Sawyer laughed. "Yes, it can certainly take some getting used to. When you've lived here a while you get a better feel for which routes are the quickest and how far in advance you have to leave home to make it to your appointments on time. It's no problem, though. I wasn't waiting long." Mr. Sawyer was a gracious host, and I was thankful that he didn't hold our tardiness against us.

I recognized a few journalists in the cafeteria and they came up to say hello. Many of the station's crew members had snuck down to the cafeteria just long enough to buy a snack, but had become caught up in talking to me and my family. They marveled at my recovery and wished me well.

"You're something of a celebrity around here, Stephen," said my mother with a smile.

"He sure is," replied Mr. Sawyer. "He's a respected journalist and the RBC family is happy to have him."

When we were finished with our meal, we took the elevator up to Mr. Sawyer's office. He closed the door behind us and offered my parents a seat. "So," he began, "you're probably all wondering what it is I've asked you to come here for?"

I nodded.

"I'd like to discuss with you a new position, Stephen. I wanted your parents here with you, because I know how much their support means to you and that you'll likely be relying on them a bit more in the future."

Mr. Sawyer stood and pulled a file from the file cabinet behind his desk. He handed it to my father. "Please look this over," he told my father. "In this file are the details of the new position."

My father began to leaf through it. As he opened the cover and read the first page, his eyes grew wide. "But, this is..."

"What is it?" asked my mother, peering over his shoulder. Her eyes grew wide as well as she read on in stunned silence.

"That's right," continued Mr. Sawyer. "The position that's just opened up is that of anchor for the nightly news. Our longtime anchor for that position is looking to retire next month. The news was sudden, but as soon as he informed me of his intention to retire, I already knew who I wanted to fill the position. Please, look over the details and discuss them."

My father and I discussed the details of the anchoring position for some time, reading through the file in its entirety. Mr. Sawyer would chime in from time to time to clarify things as we went along.

"This is an important job," said Mr. Sawyer. "Our nightly news program has a huge viewership. In some regards, I would consider this to be one of the most coveted positions here at RBC. I'm proud to offer it to you, Stephen. You're skilled and the viewers love you. I'm confident that you'll do well in this position."

I pondered his offer a moment, still too stricken with surprise to make a judgment either way. My father noticed the surprise in my expression and told Mr. Sawyer that I'd need some time to think about it. "I think he's too thrilled at the proposition to speak," he laughed.

"That's no problem," replied Mr. Sawyer. "I know that this is quite a surprise. The news came as a surprise to me as well. I don't expect Stephen to give me an answer right away. I want him to do what's best for him, so he can take his time to weigh the pros and cons of the job. He's told me many times that a job like this one has always been a dream of his."

My mother nodded. "As long as he's been a journalist he's always wanted to work as an anchor at a national station."

"Well, when would I start if I were to accept this position?" I asked.

"As I said before, the anchor is seeking to retire within a month's time. There is significant training that goes along with a job like this one, so I'd probably try and convince him to stay with us just long enough to have you fully trained. I could see you starting within two months, if everything goes according to my schedule."

"I see." I continued to scan the contents of the

file with my father. "And what about lodging? I'm just not sure that we'll be able to afford the continued transit from Detroit to New York City."

"Oh, that's not a problem," said Mr. Sawyer. "I'll arrange for you all to stay at a local hotel near the station should you choose to accept. When your training is complete, we can work with you folks to help you find a more permanent place to live."

His offer sounded great. The position would allow me to further my career, and the station was willing to help accommodate both me and my parents. It was a generous deal, all things considered. Nonetheless, I felt I needed a bit of time to consider.

"I'll tell you what," I told Mr. Sawyer, "can I get back to you tomorrow? I'd like to discuss this a bit more with my parents. I'll give you a call tomorrow morning with my answer, though."

"That's fine, Stephen. If you have any other questions, feel free to give me a call."

"I will."

He thanked us for coming and walked us out to the lobby. "I look forward to hearing from you, Stephen. And whatever you decide, please know that you have my full support."

My parents and I left the station and paid a visit to a small local cafe where we further discussed the job and its merits. My father seemed extremely excited at the prospect.

"Why didn't you just take it on the spot, Stephen! This is what you've always wanted, isn't it?"

"It is," I told him, "but things have changed. It's a big job, with a lot of responsibility. I'm not sure that I'm capable of filling this role."

My mother shook her head. "Come now, why's that? What's really changed, Stephen? You've had many struggles as of recent, but you've triumphed over every one. I'm absolutely sure that you could handle this job. In fact, you'll do more than handle it-- you'll excel. You're a great journalist; Mr. Sawyer has said so himself many times. And the viewers, Stephen-- think of them as well. They've voiced their support for you many times. I'm sure that they'd enjoy seeing you in the role of nightly anchor."

I nodded. "Perhaps. I guess I'm just a bit nervous, that's all. With all that's happened recently, I feel like this news is overwhelming. I can't make heads or tails of things. The last few months have just been surreal. I was sent to Kabul, I was injured and, now, after a lengthy recovery, I'm getting a chance to live out my dreams."

My father pinched me gently on the cheek and laughed. "Well, how about that. You're not dreaming, my boy."

"What do you think, dad? Do you think I have what it takes?"

He nodded. "More so than anyone else they could offer the job to. You're confident and talented. It's true that you've suffered some physical setbacks, but that's no reason to put limitations on your career. Plus, your mom and I will do everything we can to help you along the way. I can promise you that."

"Alright," I said. "I'm still thinking about it, but I appreciate your help. I think I'll call Mr. Sawyer tonight with my decision."

I spent the rest of the day contemplating the offer. As I'd previously done when offered the position of foreign correspondent, I sought to listen to my heart. Still, I wasn't quite sure if it was the best path for me to take. I wanted to discuss the offer with another person, and asked my mother to phone Ruth. She found Ruth's number and gave her a call for me.

"Hello, Ruth," I said into the phone as she answered.

"Stephen? Is that you? How are you?"

"I'm fine, Ruth. I was just calling to talk. Are you free at the moment?"

"I am, yes. What's on your mind, Stephen?"

I paused a moment. "Well, Mr. Sawyer at RBC headquarters has just offered me a new position. I guess one of their night-time anchors is retiring, and I've been chosen to succeed him. Mr. Sawyer met with me and my parents today to offer me the job. I'm not sure whether or not I ought to take it, though."

"Oh!" she exclaimed. "That's great news, Stephen! But why wouldn't you want to take it?"

"It's complicated, Ruth. I guess I'm just not sure whether I'm capable of filling such an important position."

She chuckled. "The Stephen Cook I worked with in Kabul wouldn't have said that. He was a confident journalist with a dream to one day anchor the news at a national station. And you know what else?"

"What?" I asked.

"Unless I'm mistaken, I'm still talking to that same Stephen Cook. Sure, you've had your fair share of setbacks, however you're still the confident, capable journalist I had the privilege of working with abroad."

"Do you really think so?" I asked.

"I do, yes. You owe it to yourself and to all of the viewers who have followed your work over the years to take this job. You have so many people in your life who are there for you-- myself included. In fact, being an anchor for the nightly news is an important job. You'll probably be in need of a personal assistant. I think I'd be available for that position if you found it necessary."

I laughed. "Well, I'd have to check out your qualifications, but I appreciate the offer."

"Whatever you do, just make sure you're happy. Life is too short to do otherwise, you know?" she said. And, more so than I'd ever known in the past, I knew she was exactly right. My life had been transformed in an instant, and because of that, I'd been given a better understanding of the fragility of life. I thought for a moment about Daniel and Michael, and how the two of them would likely have supported me as well.

"Thanks, Ruth. I'll let you know of my decision. Have a good one."

Finally, when I felt I'd come to a decision, I asked my mother to give Mr. Sawyer a call. She dialed the phone and placed it up to my ear.

"Hello?" answered Mr. Sawyer.

"Yes, Mr. Sawyer, this is Stephen Cook."

"Oh, hello, Stephen. How are you?"

"I'm fine," I replied. "I've just been thinking about your offer. I believe I've come to a decision."

"Oh? I see. What is your decision then, Stephen?"

"I'm going to follow my heart; I'm going to follow my dreams the same way I always have. I'm excited to say that I'd love to accept the position of anchor at RBC headquarters."

"That's fantastic to hear," said Mr. Sawyer. "Everyone here at the station will be happy to know that."

"I can't wait to start," I said. "Thank you for this opportunity. I really can't thank you enough for all you've done, Mr. Sawyer."

We discussed details about lodging briefly and Mr. Sawyer assured me that he would have a talk with the current anchor to make sure that he would stay

long enough for me to receive training for the position.

My training was to begin in a week's time. Until then,

my family and I were free to spend time in New York

City relaxing and sightseeing. We did just that, relishing

the opportunity to rest after the weeks of stress we'd

endured.

11

My training over the next few weeks went smoothly. The producers went to great lengths to acquaint me with every step of the anchoring process, but found me an able student even at the start. I'd spent so many years anchoring in Detroit, I felt confident in my ability to tackle the new job. It was a bigger station and, not unexpectedly, there were some major differences in the way that the folks in New York did things. Nonetheless, I adapted quickly and felt fully prepared in a matter of weeks.

The higher-ups at the station had me shadow some of the other anchors so that I could get a feel for what a typical day was like for them. I was lucky enough to follow Ben Roberts over the course of a few evenings, and I learned from him a great deal. He was patient in his instruction and he provided me with helpful hints on various matters that had helped him during his earlier days.

"Do you still get nervous?" I asked him.

"All the time," he admitted. "It doesn't matter how

long you've been doing this. If you don't get nervous before a broadcast you're losing your edge. Granted, I get less nervous now than I used to, but the point still stands. You only ever get nervous because you're afraid of doing a poor job. That shows that you're earnest, and the viewers can tell an earnest anchor from one that just reads what's on the teleprompter."

I laughed. "I'm sorry, it's just funny to hear you say that. I've been watching you on the news for so long, I just can't believe you still get nervous. You certainly don't look it."

"Well," he replied, "that calm is something you learn over time. When I first started I probably came across as a bit more nervous during broadcasts. Don't worry, though. You'll feel comfortable in this position soon."

Later in the training process, Ruth returned to the station and was once again appointed my personal assistant. She seemed thrilled to be working with me again, and proved a great help to me in completing my day-to-day work. During my training, she would scribble down countless pages of notes, and if I ever had a question about the job, she was quick to answer it. She asked me one day if I thought I was ready.

"Now that I've got you working alongside me, I feel ready to take on the world," I said.

She smiled. In Afghanistan, I'd relied quite a bit on Ruth's skills. Working with her now however, confined to my wheelchair, I found myself relying on her in an altogether greater capacity. She did not seem to mind however, and helped me in all matters with her regular cheer.

"It would seem there's only a few days left of training. I hear that tonight the anchor is going to be announcing his retirement. The station wants to keep your new position a secret until after his last day, however. Already, word of his departure has begun to spread. There's a lot of speculation out there about his replacement. I'm sure that the viewers will be surprised and happy to find out that it's you, Stephen," she said to me one afternoon during a break.

I agreed. "Yes, I imagine that news of his

retirement will come as a big surprise. The buzz about his replacement might be good for the ratings, also."

"I'll bet. The viewership for the evening news is enormous, and the people really care about the anchors. So," she said, changing the subject, "are you nervous?"

"Well," I began, "sure I am. A little bit, at least. I'll admit that I'm not nearly as anxious about the whole thing as I was at the start, though. Having learned so much about the position, I find it pretty similar to what I was doing in Detroit. For lack of a better word, I guess I feel comfortable here. Then again, there's no way to know until I actually start anchoring. I suppose time will tell."

This answer seemed to please her. "That's good to hear. I'm sure that you'll do well when the time comes for you to pick up the reigns, so to speak."

"I hope so. It's just a little daunting, knowing that my broadcast will be aired nationally."

Mr. Sawyer approached me later that same day to inquire about my training. "I expect that the staff has been helping you along, Stephen?"

"Definitely," I replied. "I feel right at home here. The staff has been very welcoming and helpful."

"Good. And how has your training been? Do you feel prepared?"

"Absolutely," I said. "I'm really looking forward to the job, in fact. It isn't all that different from the work I was doing in Detroit."

"Wonderful. Let me know if you need anything else," he said before returning to his office.

At the end of the training day, my parents came and picked me up at the station. From there, we travelled to the hotel to discuss the day's events. My parents had spent the day searching for places to live in the area, and had toured some rather nice apartments. They showed me their findings that evening during dinner.

"This apartment complex is brand new, and it has a lot of amenities. There's an elevator in the lobby, air conditioning and more. How does it look to you,

Stephen?" my father asked.

I peered at the pictures they'd taken of the model unit. "It looks really nice," I said. "Is it close to the station?"

"It is; only about a ten minute drive, if I'm not mistaken," replied my mother. "And they're also pet-friendly, so Max will be able to come along."

"That's great!" I said.

My parents seemed to enjoy living in New York. The hustle and bustle of the city kept them rather busy, however my father, who'd been in the military for so many years, found it a welcome change. He told me that he'd become somewhat bored in his retirement and that living in New York gave him an opportunity to experience many things that he'd hitherto missed out on. My mother agreed, and liked especially that we were, for the first time since I was a child, living in the same city.

Aside from the assistance they gave me on a daily basis with everyday tasks, my parents filled another very important role in my life; that of cheerleader. Their continued encouragement kept me going on days when my own confidence faltered, and I found that their presence intensified my morale. With so many important decisions laid out before me, I was in need of stability. My parents provided it in spades.

***

RBC's long-time anchor Jim Richards announced his retirement at the end of a broadcast. "I've worked for this station many years now, and, as with all goodbyes, I feel a certain sadness in leaving. Still, I look forward to my retirement, and feel confident that my successor will continue to meet the high journalistic standards that RBC is known for. Thank you all for your support over the years. Good night."

My parents and I watched in the hotel. For many viewers, I realized, it was the end of an era. The next night, I would be set to replace Mr. Richards on the nightly news, and there was no telling how the viewers would react to the sudden change in personnel. All I could do was trust Mr. Richards' assessment and hope that, in fact, I would be able to maintain the journalistic standards of the station.

After watching the broadcast I tried to go to sleep, however I found my mind cluttered with anticipation. The technical aspects of the job were simple enough; it was the viewer reaction that I could not entirely account for. Mr. Richards had been a skilled and respected anchor. I had big shoes to fill and wasn't sure if I'd be welcomed warmly by the viewers. Sure, they'd sent me messages of support many times in the past. But certainly none of them expected that I'd be replacing a familiar and well-liked anchor.

My father seemed to notice my inability to relax and sat at the edge of my bed for a while to discuss my troubles. He switched on a bedside lamp. "What's the matter, Stephen? Usually you'd be snoring away by now. Is something on your mind?"

I nodded.

"Are you nervous about the broadcast tomorrow?"

"Yeah, I guess I am. And here I thought I was

over this. I feel like a rookie. I've got a bad case of the pre-broadcast jitters, it seems."

My father chuckled. "That's not surprising, Stephen. This is a big change for you, and you'll be working for a national station. That's huge. Besides, a little nervousness isn't all that uncommon in fields like yours. You know, I hear that many musicians and actors get stage fright even when they've been performing for years. It's only natural. What's bothering you in particular? Hasn't your training been going well?"

"Yes, my training has been fine. It isn't the job itself that has me worried. I think I can handle anchoring, dad. I did it for seven years in Detroit, after all." I paused. "Mostly, I'm wondering how the viewers will react to me. They've been watching Mr. Richards for several years now. He's got a solid reputation and I just wonder whether or not I'll be able to fill his shoes."

"Sure, sure," my father replied. "That's a valid question. But you know what, Stephen? Even Jim Richards had to start somewhere. There was probably a day some years ago when he, too, was sitting awake at night, unable to sleep. Starting tomorrow night, it'll be your chance to build your own reputation. It's all right to look up to those who came before you for inspiration and advice, but don't sell yourself short. The worst thing you could do would be to try and hold yourself to someone else's standard. You're Stephen Cook, not Jim Richards. And last time I checked, being Stephen Cook has worked pretty well for you thus far."

"Maybe you're right, dad."

"Of course I am," he laughed. "Now try and get some sleep. Tomorrow's going to be a very big day."

My father's counsel put my mind at ease. In time, I managed to fall asleep. It wasn't until Ruth called late into the morning that I awoke. My mother brought the phone to me.

"Are you all ready, Stephen?" she asked me. "Tonight's the night."

"I'm as ready as I'm going to be," I replied.

***

My parents and I headed to the station, where Ruth was waiting for us. She briefed us on the day's events immediately.

"All right, tonight we'll be getting ready for the first broadcast. Stephen, we'll be introducing you tonight to all of the staff for the nightly broadcast; the sound engineers, the technicians, and all of the others. You've already met the producers, right?"

"I have, yes. A few times now, in fact," I replied.

"Good. So it would appear that, aside from a few members of the staff, you've met everybody?"

"More or less."

Ruth placed a checkmark beside an item on her checklist. "All right, so after you meet them, they'll prime you for the broadcast, set up the microphones and conduct sound tests with you. They'll probably have you rehearse the day's news a few times as well. They're all very friendly and you're used to working in a studio, so I don't expect there to be much of an issue. The show itself starts at eleven o'clock sharp. They never miss a beat, so be prepared. Once that clock in studio A strikes eleven, the cameras start rolling. Do you have any questions, Stephen?"

"Not at the moment, no. It all seems fairly straightforward."

"Good. Then I'll see you here again at about nine o'clock?"

"Will do, Ruth. Thanks."

My parents and I found ourselves free for the bulk of the day. We visited a movie theater and watched a film. From there, we ate lunch at a nice restaurant, to celebrate my new position. All the while, I sought to suppress my nerves. I wanted to enjoy this time with my family, however I found myself engaged in a constant subconscious struggle for peace of mind. I tagged along with them till nearly eight o'clock, trying to keep my mind off of the broadcast to come. Finally, at eight thirty, after I'd dressed and bathed, I made my way with them to the station.

Ruth was waiting in the lobby, chatting with

one of the staff members when we arrived. "Oh, hello, Stephen. You're here early. The crew is sure to like that. Let's head up to the studio, shall we?"

My parents and I followed Ruth to the studio. The broadcast was still a few hours away, and as a result, the studio was calmer than I'd yet seen it. Ruth sought out the producer, Randy, and asked him to introduce me to the others on the night staff.

"Good to have you aboard, Stephen. Let me round up the crew. Just a minute." He disappeared into the depths of the studio for a while and emerged with a small group of people. "This is the crew for the nightly broadcast. I've asked the crew here to get to know you a bit before we start prepping. We want you to feel comfortable with us, seeing as how we'll be working together each night."

"It's nice to meet all of you," I said. I then introduced my parents to the group as well.

The crew was very friendly. Although smaller than the crew during the earlier broadcasts, I could tell that this team was one of great skill. They navigated the studio effortlessly, preparing all of their equipment for the shoot with something not unlike absentmindedness. The whole process seemed to come naturally to them. In contrast, I felt somewhat singled out. I still wasn't comfortable in the studio, but I realized that I would become used to it in time.

Ruth read to me a few of the day's headlines. "Well, let's see here. It looks like the stock market saw an increase earlier today. There's also a story here about the war in Afghanistan." She continued reading the night's major stories to me and commenting on each. "Overall, it seems like an easy night, news-wise."

"I'm glad," I replied. "It's my first broadcast. I don't need anything too complicated to report on during my first night."

As the two of us prepared, one of the sound technicians came by and set up my microphone. He clipped it to the collar of my shirt and proceeded to do a sound check. "It looks like we've got good sound. Let me make sure it's synced up with our system." He walked to the rear of the studio and fiddled for a while with various knobs on the soundboards. "It looks good," he said, giving me a thumbs up.

One of the technicians approached me next and asked me to take a seat behind the anchor's desk. "We need to do a quick video test. Take a seat back there for me and look into the camera, if you would."

"Sure thing." I rolled towards the desk and situated myself behind it. It had been so long since I'd been in the studio, preparing for a broadcast. I recalled my final night in Detroit, and the wonderful things my old crew had done for me leading up to that last broadcast. "Is this all right, or should I move off to the side?"

"No, that's perfectly fine right there. Please look at the camera, Stephen," called out the technician.

I turned to the camera and smiled. The cameraman was instructed to adjust the lens a bit, and he moved the camera very slightly to the left. Afterward, he taped a bit of test footage, featuring my cursory rundown of the headlines. Another technician began working on the teleprompter.

Ruth walked onto the set and placed her notepad on the desk. "Well? Just like old times?" she asked.

"It really is," I said. "In many ways, it's just like being back in Detroit. I've missed this feeling more than I realized."

She smiled. "I'm sure you'll do very well tonight, Stephen. Your parents and I will be watching from the sidelines."

"And so will I," said someone else in the studio.

I turned and saw Mr. Sawyer approaching. "I wouldn't want to miss out on your first broadcast, after all."

"Hey, Mr. Sawyer. Thanks for coming," I said.

"Sure thing, Stephen. Is everything ready for the broadcast?" he asked one of the crew members.

"Not just yet; we're still setting up," they replied. "The audio and video are fine, and Stephen says he's ready. We just have a few more last-minute changes to make. Everything should be prepared shortly."

"All right. It's almost quarter till eleven, so let's hustle, everybody! You know the drill! The news starts at eleven *sharp*!"

The crew continued setting up. With only fifteen minutes left before the start of the broadcast, I studied the headlines and tried to calm myself down. I read bits of the news out loud, making sure that my voice was clear and loud. Ruth came by with a cup of water for me, and she held it to my lips so I could take a sip. "Thanks, Ruth. I was starting to feel a little parched there."

"No problem," she replied. "A little water will help keep your throat clear."

I watched the crew members rush around frantically, checking and double checking numerous devices and monitors. The producer ambled about them, nodding approvingly as they worked. "Five minutes, people. Five minutes," he called out over the chaos. At his word, things seemed to slip into a pleasant lull, and the crew members completed their preparations.

"We're all ready on this end," said one of the technicians at the soundboard.

"All right," said Randy. "We'll be starting the broadcast very shortly. Do you need anything before we begin, Stephen?" he asked me.

"No, I'm ready," I said.

"OK. Mr. Sawyer, Ruth—could you both join Stephen's parents here at the sidelines? We'll be starting very shortly."

The two of them took a seat at the edge of the set and watched with obvious excitement. My parents also looked on, both of them glowing with pride.

"One minute," called out Randy. "One minute till we start. Everybody to their positions."

The crew tensed up in preparation for the shoot. The camera zoomed in on me and the teleprompter was activated. I eyed the clock on the far end of the set and watched the seconds go by slowly.

The moments immediately prior to a shoot were always the most nerve-wracking. The final minute seemed to trickle away slowly, each second expanding and falling off of the clock stubbornly. I gazed at the camera with a smile, readying myself for the introduction. For a brief moment, I eyed my friends and family once more. They also seemed tense, probably wondering if I was still nervous. I smiled at them warmly to set their minds at ease. Everything was going to be fine.

Before I knew it, the broadcast had begun. The introduction sounded and the producer gave me my cue.

"Good evening, this is Stephen Cook, for RBC news." No sooner did the words leave my lips than I felt a surge of excitement course through my veins. I was back in the saddle, and it felt good. "I'll be replacing long-time anchor Jim Richards for the nightly broadcast. I thank you all for allowing me into your homes and hope very much that I can serve you in the years to come."

The news began to stream across the teleprompter. I read it slowly and clearly. "Tonight, we have news for you regarding the war in Afghanistan, as well as positive changes in the stock market and more."

It was surprising just how easily it all came back to me. It had been months since my last broadcast in

Detroit, however I'd managed to retain my anchoring skills. I felt, in some ways, as though I'd never left.

The broadcast lasted an hour. During the commercial breaks, Ruth would creep onto the set to make sure I didn't need anything. "How's it going for you, Stephen? Do you need anything before we're back on air?"

"No, I'm fine. Thanks for asking, Ruth."

"You're doing great, by the way. You seem very relaxed. Watching you from the sidelines I never would have expected this to be your first day. You look like an old pro!"

I smiled. "Thanks."

I signed off at the end of the broadcast and joined everyone else in the studio. The crew came by to congratulate me on a successful first broadcast and Mr. Sawyer agreed. "Stephen, that was fantastic. You did even better than I expected. That was a very professional broadcast, and I look forward to seeing more."

"Thanks for saying so, Mr. Sawyer. It was enjoyable for me, and I thank you for the opportunity to anchor this program."

My parents approached me as well. They wrapped me in an embrace and relayed to me their surprise. "I thought you were nervous, Stephen! It sure didn't look like it," said my father.

"Well, what can I say? Your advice helped me clear my head, dad."

Emerging from the studio into the bustling night, I felt more alive than I had in a great while. A pale moon floated in the black sky, casting a dull, beautiful glow over the world below. The cool breeze carried with it the sounds of traffic and the clatter of passing pedestrians. In a way, the city seemed alive. The crew members laughed and carried on jovially as we entered the restaurant.

Despite the late hour, many of us decided to visit a small restaurant near the station to celebrate. My parents, Ruth, Mr. Sawyer and numerous members of the crew decided to come along, and we shared a fine meal.

That evening, I realized something important. The people at the station were more than just colleagues. They were like family to me, and in the months since that first broadcast, I've come to regard them as some of my dearest friends.

***

It's been a few months since I began anchoring the nightly news at RBC's main station. The viewer response has been overwhelmingly positive, and I found that many viewers were delighted to learn that I was the new anchor. As before, the viewers took to social media to share their feelings, and I found myself taken aback by their kindness. Many of them had enjoyed my work in Kabul, and looked forward to my future work on the nightly news.

My parents and I have since relocated to New York City, and are living in a nice apartment building. And of course, Max came along as well. In my off time, my parents and I have been able to enjoy the many things that New York has to offer; visiting museums, great restaurants and more. Max also enjoys going for walks with my parents at Central Park.

I had the opportunity to visit the Detroit affiliate once more, and was welcomed by all of my old crew members. At first, many of them approached me nervously, feeling that I was something of a celebrity. They warmed up to me quickly however, when they realized that I was still the same person. Many of them expressed that they'd been worried about me during my hospitalization, and that they were happy to see that I'd made a recovery. We had a small celebration at the old station, and I was relieved to find all of my old friends were still there.

"You've made all of us here very proud, Stephen. You're an inspiration to all of us," said Dave during my visit.

Throughout my career, I've experienced many things. I worked hard in college and took a job in Detroit. I honed my craft and worked as an anchor at the RBC affiliate station for seven years. From there, I was given a fantastic opportunity to work in Kabul. During my time there, I met many wonderful individuals and immersed myself in the local culture. I also went through a great physical change in Kabul. The blast that left me paralyzed has not been a negative thing, however.

Perhaps it sounds strange to call such an event positive, however the blast in Afghanistan that left me paralyzed opened my mind to something I'd hitherto neglected to realize. My paralysis, however inconvenient at times, has taught me about my limitations. Or rather, it has taught me that I haven't any. In my earlier days as a journalist, though confident, I had imposed various limitations on myself and at times doubted my ability to improve. My disability has awakened me to my true potential however, and for that I am thankful. My paralysis has not at all affected my ability to follow my dreams.

In the time since my recovery, I've learned that there is nothing outside of my reach. With enough discipline and the assistance of my friends and family, I've found that anything is possible. Although I'm very pleased with my current position, it's hard to say what the future will bring. In a few years, perhaps I'll seek out another position; something that will challenge me further. Despite my success, I'm always looking for ways to challenge myself and improve.

ABOUT THE AUTHOR

A native of Metro Detroit, Charlie Kadado, wrote his first published piece at age 7. At 15, he wrote and published his first novel, Sacrifice: Reporting in Kabul.

As a Scholastic News Kid Reporter, Charlie discovered a passion in journalism. He is the host of a television program at HMD Multimedia in Detroit and a freelance journalist for local and national print and television affiliates.

An enthusiastic orator, Charlie founded the Want. Work. Win Motivational Campaign in 2010 with the intent to motivate young people across the state. He is also a dedicated public servant and recipient of the Gold President's Volunteer Service Award from President Obama and Special Tribute from the State of Michigan.